"You're mad now, but you'll get over it in a day or two. Then you'll have a new guy in love with you," Kristi said to her best friend.

"Not this time," Molly declared. "This day is going to be entered into my diary as 'The day I swore off boys.' "

"I'll bet you're wrong," Kristi said.

"You're on. Just name the stakes."

Kristi gave her a sidelong glance. "OK, Kincaid. School is out in one more week, and we've got the whole summer ahead of us. If you haven't had a date or become interested in a boy by the time school starts again in the fall, I'll be your slave for a month. But if you do find a new boyfriend, then you have to be my slave."

"What do you mean by slave?" Molly asked.

"Whoever loses has to do whatever the winner asks—homework and chores and favors and lending clothes and all that kind of stuff."

"You've got a bet!" Molly agreed with enthusiasm.

Bantam Sweet Dreams Romances
Ask your bookseller for the books you have missed

# No More Boys

## Charlotte White

**BANTAM BOOKS**
TORONTO • NEW YORK • LONDON • SYDNEY • AUCKLAND

RL 5, IL age 11 and up

NO MORE BOYS
*A Bantam Book / June 1986*

*Cover photo by Pat Hill*

ISBN 0-553-25643-2

*Published simultaneously in the United States and Canada*

*Bantam Books are published by Bantam Books, Inc. Its trademark,
consisting of the words "Bantam Books" and the portrayal of a
rooster, is registered in U.S. Patent and Trademark Office and in
other countries. Marca Registrada. Bantam Books, Inc., 666 Fifth
Avenue, New York, New York 10103.*

Printed and bound in Great Britain by Hunt Barnard Printing Ltd.

O   0 9 8 7 6 5 4 3 2 1

# No More Boys

# Chapter One

"Uh, Molly, I've changed my mind. Let's go," Kristi Jackson said, pulling on Molly Kincaid's arm. Molly had just stepped through the door of Skip's, a fast-food restaurant. Molly swung around to face her best friend, curiosity reflected in her large brown eyes.

"What's the matter?" Molly asked. "We just got here."

"I know. But I've lost my appetite," Kristi said. She tried to shrug casually, but it came off looking phony. There was also a nervous edge to her voice. Kristi turned to walk out of the restaurant. "Come on," she implored, looking back at Molly.

"I don't get it," Molly said. "Only two minutes ago you told me that Skip's french fries were the only thing that could save you from starvation."

"OK. So I exaggerated a little. Please, Molly, let's just go," Kristi whispered.

Molly shook her head and started to follow Kristi out the door. But suddenly she realized that Kristi was hiding something—or some-one—from her.

Very slowly Molly turned around to look at everyone in the crowded restaurant, the favor-ite high-school hangout in Oak Park, Ohio. The first person she saw was her boyfriend, Robert Prentiss. They had been going out for almost a year, since they'd met the previous summer at the beach. Robert was a year older than she was, and he was cute, smart, and popular. Robert was the perfect boyfriend—every girl's dream.

Molly's gaze stopped on the person in the booth with Robert. Linda McCall, a sopho-more with long, black hair and a body all the boys talked about, was staring raptly at Rob-ert. The problem was that Robert was staring right back. He was clasping one of Linda's hands in his and gazing deeply into her eyes. Molly recognized the look on his face. After all, Robert had looked at her that way many times.

When had he stopped? Molly wondered. She

hadn't thought about it until just then. When had he gotten tired of her? She hadn't even noticed.

Between clenched teeth, Molly muttered, "I can't believe it—"

"Calm down," Kristi interrupted softly. "I tried to get you out of here. It'll be OK. You can talk to him later. Let's just go."

"No, I'll talk now," Molly said. "Let me handle this *my* way, Kristi."

Molly knew Kristi had just been trying to help. The two girls had been best friends since kindergarten even though they weren't very much alike. Kristi was short, dark, timid, and easily embarrassed. Molly was tall, blond, outgoing, and hot-tempered. When Molly was mad, she reacted. And at that moment, Molly was mad. She tugged Robert's class ring off her finger and started across the floor with even, purposeful strides.

"Molly, don't—" Kristi called after her. But the warning was lost. Once Molly Kincaid started something, she finished it. By the time she reached the booth where Robert and Linda were sitting, everyone at Skip's had noticed her—everyone except Robert and Linda. The restaurant was silent.

"Robert, I think you might be needing this," Molly said. Her voice rang out in the stillness.

Robert turned just in time to see her drop the ring on the table. It clattered noisily against the Formica surface.

Robert dropped Linda's hand and sprang to his feet. "Molly, you don't understand. I—"

"Save it, Robert," Molly interrupted. "Come by my house tonight around eight. I'll have the rest of your things ready for you. Don't bother to ring the door bell. Everything will be in a box on the porch."

Molly tossed back her shoulder-length blond hair and strode to the door, where Kristi waited for her. The jukebox blared in the background. Some of the kids stared at Molly openly. But most of them were more discreet, acting as if they hadn't noticed anything unusual. A murmur of conversation swept over the booths in the restaurant, but Molly didn't care what anyone thought or said.

The two girls walked across the parking lot toward Kristi's battered little car. Molly glanced at her friend. Kristi's face was very pale, and her expression was sympathetic but wary.

"Hey, Kris," Molly said with a short laugh, "cheer up. *I'm* the one who just caught her boyfriend with another girl."

Kristi was silent for a moment. Then she said, "I can't believe you did that—breaking

4

up in public. I could never do anything like that. It would be so embarrassing."

"Embarrassing?" Molly laughed again. "Of course it was. It was also embarrassing to see my boyfriend holding hands with another girl. What would you have done in my place? Would you have tiptoed away as if you hadn't noticed them and then talked to Robert later?"

"Probably," Kristi replied. "I hate scenes."

Molly shrugged. "To each her own. *Robert* made the scene. I just did what I had to do. I'd rather stand up and say what I think than burst into tears."

"I'm not saying you're wrong," Kristi said as she slipped behind the wheel of the car. "I'm just saying I could never do what you did. Guess that makes me a wimp." Kristi looked over at Molly. She spoke quietly. "Molly, you're with *me* now. You can cry or do whatever you want."

Molly glared at the dashboard. None of the gauges in the old car worked, not even the gas gauge. It had always registered empty, so Kristi stopped at a gas station every other day.

"I don't need to cry," Molly declared. "I'm feeling great. I'm free. This is the best thing that's happened to me in ages."

"You're lying. You look lousy," Kristi countered.

5

Molly wouldn't look at her. "OK, so I'm lying. But I'm not going to cry. Robert isn't worth it. Did you know about this before today?"

Kristi nodded slightly. "I've been hearing rumors, but I didn't believe them. Until today, that is."

"You know what burns me?" Molly asked. "The sneakiness. He could have *told* me he was interested in someone else. I'd have understood that. But leading me on and letting me find out this way—that's low. I wouldn't have liked to hear him say the words, but if he had to break up with me, I would have preferred a more honest approach."

"I guess it wouldn't be easy to tell someone that you wanted to break up," Kristi mused. "Besides, maybe Robert didn't really want to break up. Maybe he just wanted—"

"To have a girl on each arm. No way. I'm done with Robert Prentiss. In fact, I'm done with boys. Period. No more dates," Molly announced. She sat back in her seat and folded her arms.

Before Kristi could answer, the car made a sudden, violent noise. "I hate this beast," said Kristi. "But it was either a new old car or a new bedroom. I think I chose wrong. Since we're supposed to share this heap, you'd think Ben would try to fix it up. I mean, isn't that

6

what boys are supposed to do, mess with cars? But not *my* brother. He's always off on some crusade to save the bald eagle or the whale or something like that. He doesn't even know which end of a wrench to use."

She glanced over at Molly, who was staring morosely out the window. "Sorry. I didn't mean to change the subject, I know how upset you are. You don't mean what you're saying, Molly. You've been 'in love' with someone ever since I've known you, starting with Todd Marshall in kindergarten. You're mad at Robert now, but you'll get over it in a day or two. Then you'll have a new guy in love with you."

"Not this time," Molly declared. "This is going to be entered in my diary in red letters as 'The day I swore off boys.'"

"I'll bet you on that one," Kristi said.

"You're on. Name the stakes."

"You'll have your eye on someone else within a week, or I'll buy you a pizza."

Molly groaned. "Come on, Jackson. I thought you were sure of yourself. I thought you wanted to bet. If we're going to have a wager, let's make it worthwhile."

Kristi gave her a sidelong glance. "OK, Kincaid. You asked for it. School is out in one more week, and we've got the whole summer ahead of us. If you haven't had a date or become interested in a boy by the time we're juniors in the fall, then I'll be your slave for the month of September. And, if you find a boyfriend, then you have to be my slave."

"What do you mean by slave?" Molly asked.

"Whoever loses has to do whatever the winner asks—homework and chores and favors and lending clothes and all that kind of stuff."

"Sounds too good to pass up. You're on," Molly said.

"You're sure?" Kristi prodded her.

"I'm sure," Molly told her. "This will be easy."

"Good. It's settled then." Kristi sighed. "Do you have time to go by my house before you go home? I want you to see my room now that it's totally finished."

All Molly wanted to do was be by herself for a while. She felt worse about Robert than she'd let on. But she couldn't think of a good excuse to go home immediately. "Sure, if you won't mind driving me home afterward. I can't stay long. Mom has some stuff she wants me to do," Molly added lamely.

"I'll be glad to take you home, if the beast'll start again, that is," Kristi said agreeably.

A short time later, Kristi steered the little car into her driveway. The Jackson house, tidy and spotless inside and out, didn't seem to go with the car Kristi and Ben drove. More in keeping with the house was the sparkling sedan with the velvety interior that was parked in the garage.

Kristi led Molly to her newly decorated room. A few days earlier the last workman had picked up his tools and gone, leaving behind a beautiful ivory-and-blue bedroom. Kristi was obviously proud of the results. Molly looked around at the new wallpaper, thick, pale carpet, and puffy, quilted bedspread.

"It's beautiful," Molly said sincerely. "It's like a picture out of a magazine."

And it was. Not a thing was out of place. Molly mentally contrasted Kristi's newly decorated room with her own.

Molly lived in a happy jumble of posters, books, discarded clothes, tissue boxes, and other stray items. Although Kristi's room *was* beautiful, Molly knew she couldn't live in it. To her, it had no character, no atmosphere. Molly's room was her sanctuary. What good was a place of refuge, she thought, if she had to worry about messing up the bedspread?

"I'd love to have a room like this," she told Kristi. "But you know me. I'd have it junked up in no time." She looked at her watch. "Well, I hate to run so quickly, Kristi, but duty calls."

9

"Sure, I understand," Kristi agreed. "And if you want to talk later—you know, about Robert—give me a call."

"Thanks. I appreciate it."

They walked in silence from Kristi's room to the kitchen, where Mrs. Jackson was bustling around, preparing dinner.

"Mom, I'll be back in just a few minutes. I'm going to take Molly home," Kristi said.

"Did you forget, dear? You're supposed to go next door to baby-sit Gretchen. The Bennetts have to leave pretty soon," Mrs. Jackson said, stirring a cream sauce with a whisk.

Kristi put one hand on her forehead. "Darn, I did forget! Mom, I promised Molly I'd take her home. Do you think I have time for that?"

"That's all right," Molly said quickly, noting Mrs. Jackson's hesitation. "It isn't that far. I don't mind walking."

"Nonsense," said Mrs. Jackson. "There's no need for that. Ben can take you home." She called, "Ben!"

"What?" came the muffled reply from behind Ben's closed door.

"Please come out here, dear. I need you to do something."

Ben Jackson, just a year older than Kristi and Molly, had transferred to a private school across town at the beginning of his junior year. Kristi had said that it was because he wanted to get into an Ivy League university, and he thought that St. Paul Academy would prepare him for it better. Privately, Molly thought the academy kids were a pretty dull bunch. They never attended sports events against Oak Park High, and their teams almost never won when they *did* play. Kristi had been offered the chance to transfer for her junior year, and Molly had been relieved when she had decided not to.

Ben stretched and yawned as he came into the kitchen in a rumpled T-shirt and jeans. His dark hair was ruffled, and Molly wondered if he had been sleeping. His school was already finished.

"What do you want, Mom?" Ben asked.

"Please drive Molly home, dear," Mrs. Jackson said. "Kristi has to baby-sit at the Bennetts', and I can't get away from the kitchen just yet."

Molly blushed. Ben treated Molly like another little sister. He'd always had to cart her and Kristi around. But lately, it hadn't happened so often. She felt a little silly about Mrs. Jackson's request, but Ben didn't seem to mind at all.

"Sure," he said. "Ready, Molly?"

"I'm ready," she replied.

"Call me tonight, or I'll just see you tomorrow," Kristi said as Molly left. "Don't forget our bet. I'm looking forward to having a slave next September."

"You should look forward to *becoming* a slave next September," Molly said. "I've told you—I'm a changed woman." She turned and followed Ben out to the driveway.

Ben's long legs carried him to the beat-up car well ahead of Molly. By the time she was seated, he was settled behind the wheel and watching her with open curiosity. "What's all this about a bet?" he asked.

"Oh, nothing," Molly replied. She wished Kristi hadn't said anything in front of Ben.

Backing the car out of the driveway, he grinned and said, "Come on now, don't be bashful. Tell brother Ben how you've changed."

"Well, if you *have* to know, I've sworn off guys. I'm through with dating and everything that goes along with it," Molly said.

"You?" Ben asked skeptically. "You've had a boyfriend ever since I've known you. What happened? Did you and Robert Prentiss have a little difference of opinion?"

"More than a little one," she admitted. "In fact, we're finished. But I don't care."

"You don't?"

"No, I don't. I've decided there's no future in dating. From now on I'm going to devote my time to more worthwhile things," Molly declared.

"Oh, you are?" he asked. "Like what?" Ben sounded amused. But Ben had always teased her and Kristi.

"I have to think it over. But I'm going to do something. Maybe I'll volunteer to be a candy striper at the hospital," she said. *That'll show him I'm serious,* Molly thought.

They remained silent until Ben pulled the car up in front of Molly's house. As she turned to him to thank him for the ride, she saw that he was smiling.

"Now you're acting just like Kristi," she burst out. "You don't believe me. Well, I'll show you. I'll show you and everyone else, including Robert Prentiss."

"Good luck," Ben said genially. "You know," he added, "there may be a way I can help you out. I'll check on it and let you know."

"What is it?" Molly asked skeptically.

"I said I'll check and let you know. I don't want to get your hopes up and then let you down. See you later, Molly."

"Thanks for the ride," Molly answered. She got out of the car.

"I hope you win that bet," Ben said.

"You *do*?" Molly asked, poking her head back into the car. "What difference does it make to you?"

Ben shrugged. "Oh, I don't know. I'd just like to believe there are a few kids in Oak Park capable of breaking out of the popularity trap." He waved and backed the car out of the driveway.

His words puzzled Molly. She sighed and looked at her house with reluctance. Her mom would be able to tell something was wrong. She'd probably ask questions, and Molly was in no mood to answer questions and talk about Robert Prentiss. Squaring her shoulders, Molly walked into the house.

# Chapter Two

Molly closed the door behind her. The house was silent. Walking into the kitchen, she spotted a note stuck to the refrigerator with a magnet.

> Molly,
> Dad had to take a business associate and his wife to dinner in Cleveland, and he wanted me to go along. We won't be late. There's stew in the slow cooker for your supper. Please feed Claude.
>
> > Love,
> > Mom

Molly was relieved. As much as she loved her parents, she needed to be alone just then.

Molly made her way down the hall and into her room. The first thing she saw was a large framed photograph of Robert. She flipped it over, then flung herself down on one of the twin beds.

There, in her own room, she could finally cry. She had gone out with Robert for almost a year. She had trusted him completely. Not only would she miss him; his betrayal was a real blow to her pride.

As Kristi had pointed out to her, Molly had always had boyfriends. It wasn't the first time she had broken up with someone. It was, however, the first breakup *she* hadn't initiated. Molly had always been the one to call the shots. She didn't like being dropped. She didn't like it at all.

Molly was still crying when she felt Claude, her fat, gray cat, jump on the bed. He rubbed against her and purred for her attention. Molly smiled in spite of herself and smoothed the big cat's soft, thick fur. He sat down on her chest, looked her directly in the eye, and continued to purr.

"You purr-box," she said affectionately. "Are you trying to comfort me, or are you just reminding me it's time to eat?"

Moving the cat off her chest, she sat up and looked around. The cluttered, comfortable room was filled with things that reminded her of Robert Prentiss.

"Time for action," she said aloud.

She went to the basement and found a huge cardboard box. Back in her room, she began to systematically strip the walls and furniture of everything that Robert had given her. She placed Robert's letter jacket and picture into the box and added the collection of notes and letters she had saved, plus all the presents he had given her. She didn't know what Robert would do with the stuffed animals, half-used bottles of cologne, and gold chains and bracelets, and she didn't care. As long as *she* didn't have to look at them!

When the task was completed, the room looked better, and Molly felt better. She hummed all the way down the stairs as she lugged the big box to the porch.

Claude stayed with her every step of the way. After she had dumped the box on the porch, she rubbed his head and said, "OK, you win. Supper time." She opened a can of cat food for him and spooned it into his bowl.

Molly didn't expect to be hungry. But, to her surprise, she was. She filled a bowl with stew and buttered a slice of bread.

When Molly was done eating, she cleaned up the kitchen and went into the family room, glancing at her watch. It was nearly eight o'clock. She wondered if Robert would really come to get his things. Maybe he'd want to talk to her, to explain what had happened— that Linda meant nothing to him and that he wanted to patch things up.

Molly didn't want to patch things up. She meant what she'd said—she was through with boys in general, and Robert in particular. Still, there would be *some* satisfaction in watching him apologize and make excuses. She could just hear him: "Molly, you know how much you mean to me. The thing with Linda wasn't anything. It took almost losing you to bring me to my senses. Please give me another chance!"

A few minutes after eight she heard Robert's car pull up in front of her house. She walked over to the window and hid behind the curtains so he wouldn't see her. Robert glanced furtively from side to side, then stepped up on the porch. Molly waited for the door bell to ring, wondering what she would say to him. But nothing happened. She peeked out again. Robert, with the box in his arms, was headed back to his car. When he opened the door, Molly saw someone else in the car—a girl with long, dark hair. It was Linda.

There was an ache in her stomach. *So much*

*for fantasies*, she thought. Robert wasn't going to tell her he wanted her back. He wasn't even going to apologize for the way he had been sneaking around.

Molly looked at herself in the hall mirror. *I'm a total mess*, she thought. Her blond hair was tangled, her face was blotchy from crying, and her eyes were red. Taking a crumpled tissue from her jeans pocket, she blew her nose. She looked herself squarely in the eye and said, "You would have taken him back, you know. You really would have."

The admission wasn't an easy one for Molly to make—and she'd never have told anyone. With a much stronger resolve than before, she promised herself that she really would stay away from boys and dating. From then on, Molly Kincaid was going to be noble, high-minded, and dedicated to worthy causes. She wasn't sure what those worthy causes would be, but she would figure that out later. Someone out there needed her. She just had to find her cause and devote herself to it.

Molly wrote a note to her parents and put it on the refrigerator. "I'm in my room studying for my psychology test. Hope you had a nice time. The stew was delicious. See you at breakfast. Love, Molly."

She wasn't sure if that would keep her folks

from poking their heads into her bedroom to say good night. Molly knew she would have to tell her parents about Robert in the morning. But for one night she wanted to be alone.

After changing into her nightgown and plopping down on her bed, Molly had another good, long cry. Then, feeling swollen and soggy, she propped herself up against the pillows and devoted her full attention to studying psychology.

In the morning, she felt a little better. Not a lot better, just a little.

"Robert and I broke up yesterday," she told her parents over the breakfast table. She hoped she sounded more together than she felt. *Hiding a broken heart requires terrific acting*, Molly thought.

Her parents exchanged glances as if they were trying to decide what to say.

"Well, Robert lasted a lot longer than your other boyfriends," her dad said heartily. "He's a nice boy. Mutual agreement? No hard feelings between you?"

"That's it, Dad," Molly lied. "No use being emotional and yelling and crying. It's silly, at my age, to be tied down to just one person."

Barbara Kincaid's voice was even and smooth. "That's what I always thought, dear. I didn't have anything against Robert. I just thought you should play the field and not get too serious. There's plenty of time for falling in love and settling down later on."

"You're right, Mom," Molly agreed. "But I've decided not to get involved again. There's no future in dating."

Mr. Kincaid laughed and reached across the table to pat her hand. "You'll change your mind, Molly, when the right guy comes along. Falling in love and marrying are a natural part of life."

Molly shook her head vehemently. "Not for me. What's so great about it? Look at the divorce statistics. It's all too risky and point-less. I've decided to dedicate myself to more important matters."

Her parents exchanged looks again, and Molly knew she hadn't fooled them with her little speech. She was upset, and they knew it. Molly hoped that they wouldn't try to talk about it.

"That's fine," her dad said in a voice that was a little too jovial. "There are a lot of impor-tant matters to be seen to. What did you have in mind?"

"You sound like Ben Jackson," she muttered.

"What does Kristi's brother have to do with this?" Mrs. Kincaid asked.

"He doesn't have *anything* to do with it. He just asked me that same question, that's all."

"That's a natural reaction," Mr. Kincaid replied, shrugging.

"Anyway, I have to think about what I'm going to do," Molly said. "Maybe I'll be a candy striper at the hospital."

"I thought the sight of blood made you sick," her mother commented.

"Pessimism," Molly said. "That's all I ever get. OK, I'm not crazy about blood. But I don't think they let candy stripers perform surgery. They just pass out flowers and mail and read the newspapers to old people. Anyway, Ben said he had something in mind for me. He wouldn't tell me what, but it's bound to be noble and important. You know how Ben is."

They knew. Everyone in Oak Park knew. Ever since he was a little kid, Ben Jackson had been all over town collecting donations and passing out literature for one cause or another. When other boys were collecting baseball cards, Ben had been out crusading for the survival of anything or anyone that was threatened.

"How's Ben doing at St. Paul Academy?" her dad asked.

"Beats me," replied Molly. "I never ask, and Kristi never tells me. Ben's always been kind of quiet. It would be funny if he knew of something for me to get involved in. I can't wait to find out what it is. But if that doesn't work out, I'll still find *something* to do this summer."

"If you want suggestions, you could start with cleaning your room," her mom said.

Molly rolled her eyes. Then she stood up and carried her plate and glass to the sink. "Actually, I got a good start on my room last night. I cleared away a lot of junk. Old photographs and stuff."

Molly saw that her mother knew exactly what she meant by junk. They exchanged a long look that said more than words ever could. Barbara Kincaid gave her daughter a quick hug.

"I'm proud of you, Molly," she said softly. "And I know you'll find something worthwhile to do this summer."

# Chapter Three

The following day was probably the worst one Molly had had since she'd entered high school. She ran into Robert and Linda—together—everywhere. Her friends suddenly stopped talking whenever she appeared. And jokes about her bet with Kristi were being exchanged everywhere.

"Am I getting paranoid?" she muttered to Kristi between classes, "or is everyone talking about me?"

Kristi laughed but then smiled sympathetically and said, "A little of both. A lot of people *are* talking about you, but not everyone. Word gets around, Molly, and you and Robert were quite an item for a long time. And some of the kids were at Skip's when you dropped the ring on the table. But don't worry, talk will die down."

"The sooner the better," Molly mumbled. "Why did you tell people about our bet?"

Kristi looked sheepish. "Sorry, I thought it would help my chances of winning if some of the guys knew how much is riding on your next date."

"Thanks a lot," Molly muttered.

At home that night Molly looked through the classified section of the newspaper for worthy causes. She couldn't find anything. It wasn't going to be easy to find the person or organization that needed her services. While she was putting the paper back, the telephone rang.

"It's for you," her dad called. "Some *boy*," he added triumphantly.

Molly tried to look unconcerned, but as she approached the telephone, her heart was pounding. What if it was *Robert* on the phone? What would she say?

"Hello," she said tentatively.

"Molly, this is Ben."

Molly felt both disappointed and relieved. Ben definitely wasn't Robert. "Oh, hi, Ben," she said flatly.

"Uh, I have something I need to talk to you

about. You want to come over, you want me to come over there, or you want to meet somewhere for a soda? It doesn't matter to me," he added.

Molly thought he sounded nervous—as if he were asking for a date or something. Then she dismissed the idea. Ben was just awkward. He was great when he wanted people to understand one of his causes, but he wasn't very good at conversation.

"Can't you tell me over the phone?" Molly asked him.

"I'd rather not."

Molly sighed into the receiver. "OK. Mom wanted me to pick up a couple of things for her at the grocery store, anyway. I'll meet you at Skip's in fifteen minutes. Then I'll get her stuff after we talk."

"Fine. You *are* still serious about wanting something worthwhile to do, aren't you?" Ben asked.

"I am, but—" Molly said.

"Great. See you in fifteen minutes," Ben interrupted and hung up.

"What did you want to tell me?" she asked Ben when they were both seated at Skip's, their soft drinks in front of them. He was neatly dressed—in jeans and a cotton, button-down shirt, but he still looked rumpled. Ben was so different from Robert that comparing them was just silly, she thought.

"I've been thinking about majoring in psychology when I go to college," Ben began.

Molly stared at him. What did that have to do with her?

"Someday I'd like to be a guidance counselor for troubled kids. To help me make up my mind if that's what I really want to do with my life, I'm going to be working at the city park this summer. It'll give me some experience with kids, so I'll know if I can take it or not."

Molly nodded. She'd heard of the city park summer program.

"That's nice, Ben," she said. "It'll be good to get a chance like that. It'd be awful to get a degree in something and then find out you didn't like it once you started working."

"That's what I think. Anyway, Mrs. Abbott, the woman who heads the program, told me they needed another counselor. If you're interested in the job, I can put you in touch with her. I'm pretty sure you can have it, if you want it."

Molly poked at the ice in her drink with the straw. "What would I have to do?" she asked. "You know, what kind of work?"

Ben shrugged. "I figured I'd just show up the first day and play it by ear."

"Oh, Ben. You must have some idea what we'd do," Molly said.

His slow, lazy grin was maddening. "The program is for kids from four to ten years old. It's free, so it's very popular. Parents know that they can trust us with their kids, and they don't have to pay baby-sitters. The program runs from eight in the morning to three in the afternoon, and each child brings a bag lunch from home. We're there to teach them games, and help them with crafts—stuff like that. Mrs. Abbott will give us our specific assignments each day. She'll have all the activities planned," he told her.

Molly looked down at the table. Water dripped from her cup into a little puddle. She remembered seeing the kids in the park the previous summer. As she recalled, there were *lots* of them. How would she do?

As if he read her thoughts, Ben continued talking, "I've never been good at talking to people. I've always been more of a thinker than a talker. But if I'm going to help these kids, I have to communicate with them. That's where you can help me. *And* the kids. Mrs. Abbott said she wanted someone who's outgoing and—"

"Talkative," Molly said, finishing his sentence. "That's why you thought of me? Because I talk so much?"

Ben grinned at her across the table and didn't bother to deny her accusation. "People like you, Molly. You're friendly. You can always think of something to say. Maybe I can learn from watching you. Kristi told me that you were the one who managed to get a salad bar put in Oak Park High's cafeteria. I mean, you know how to get things done."

Molly shook her head. "I don't know, Ben," she said slowly. "This wasn't exactly what I had in mind. I want to do something important. But being a glorified baby-sitter for a bunch of little kids? I don't want to spend the summer teaching kids to finger paint and play games."

"For the most part, these are kids who don't have a lot going for them at home. No one plays with them much or bothers to teach them things," Ben said. "Mrs. Abbott says great things have come out of this program. She says the kids love it, and they gain more confidence in themselves during the summer than they do the rest of the year. You can't just think of this as baby-sitting, Molly. You have to think of it as helping young feet get started on the path of life."

Molly looked directly into Ben's clear gray eyes and smiled. "I thought you said you weren't good at talking, Ben," she teased. "You should hear yourself. You sound as convincing as the best lawyer summing up his case."

Ben's face flushed with color. "I guess I got a bit carried away," he mumbled.

"That's OK. You almost have me convinced," Molly said.

"The pay isn't much," he continued earnestly. "The program is financed through grants, and the budget is tight. We'll only get minimum wage, and we probably won't work a full forty-hour week. But at least you'd make *some* money."

Molly was on the verge of saying money didn't matter when she thought of all the new clothes she could buy. She could have a wardrobe that would make Robert Prentiss sit up and take notice. *Not that he matters,* Molly told herself. "I'll think about it," she said.

"Don't think too long," he cautioned. "The program starts in two weeks, and Mrs. Abbott needs to have someone lined up."

"Oh, all right," Molly said.

Their soft drinks gone, Ben and Molly got up, paid, and walked out of the restaurant. Molly looked over at Ben. His dark hair was too long and needed combing. But when he'd been talking about the summer job, his face had lit up, making his eyes flash with enthusiasm.

For as long as Molly had known him, Ben always managed to look windblown and wrinkled. He never looked really sloppy, just unconcerned, as if getting dressed were an afterthought. Ben always managed to make Molly feel uncomfortable about herself. She cared about ecology and endangered species and underprivileged children. But while Ben was out doing something about those things, Molly had been hanging out with her friends.

But she had opened her mouth and said she was going to change and dedicate herself to noble causes. She supposed this was as good a place to start as any.

"OK," she said with a sigh.

"OK, what?" Ben asked.

"I'll take that job. That is, if Mrs. Abbott approves of me," Molly added.

"You mean that?" Ben said jubilantly.

Molly nodded.

"Terrific! I just know she'll approve of you. Listen, we can go by her place right now. I just spoke to her on the phone a little while ago, so I know she's home. What do you think?" Ben asked.

"Maybe tomorrow will be better. I still have to get some stuff for my mother."

"It'll only take a few minutes," Ben said, coaxing her. Molly finally agreed to go with him in his car. She knew he wasn't going to give her a chance to change her mind. *This could be one of the most insane things I've done*, Molly thought. She didn't know anything about taking care of kids or working with them. Claude was the only living being she had ever had to care for, and he didn't need much more than food and water. Molly had the feeling that taking care of a park full of kids was going to be a lot more difficult.

# Chapter Four

Ben pulled his battered car up in front of a tidy white house.

"This is where Mrs. Abbott lives," he announced. He got out of the car and bounded up the sidewalk to the front door without a backward glance. Molly was struggling with her door. The handle came off in her hand, and it was, she found, virtually impossible to open the door without it. She scooted over to the driver's side and crawled out through that door.

"There you are," Ben said, beaming at her when she joined him on the front stoop. "What took you so long?"

She gave him a bright, fake smile. "I was hunting for a way to get out of your car. You see, there was this little matter of a broken door handle."

"Oh. I forgot about that," Ben said, embarrassed.

The door opened before he could add anything else. They were greeted by a tiny, smiling woman. She was thin, with a face full of freckles, and had graying, red hair. *She has to be Mrs. Abbott*, Molly thought. She positively radiated energy. She was dressed in a sweat suit and running shoes. *If anyone can handle a hundred or so kids, this lady can*, Molly decided.

"Mrs. Abbott," Ben began, "this is Molly Kincaid. I talked to you about her earlier today. We wanted to come right over."

"Fine, fine. Nice to meet you, Molly." Mrs. Abbott said.

She put out a freckled hand, and Molly took it. Her grip was quick and firm.

"Come on in. I just made some iced tea," she offered.

She led them through her bright house. It was the most comfortable-looking house Molly had ever seen. Everything was tidy, yet lived in and homey.

"I love your house, Mrs. Abbott," Molly said.

"So do I," Mrs. Abbott replied firmly. She led them onto a sun porch that was closed in with glass on three sides. The furniture was white wicker, and the cushions and rugs were grass green and lemon yellow. On a table in the corner stood a pitcher of tea and several glasses.

Ben started right in as he sat down in one of the chairs.

"I think Molly would be great for the camp job, Mrs. Abbott. She's friendly, outgoing, well organized—all the things I'm not."

"I've told you a hundred times to call me Pat," Mrs. Abbott told Ben. "It always makes me feel positively ancient to be called Mrs. Abbott. Of course, in your eyes, fifty probably *is* ancient."

Pat looked closely at Molly, then back at Ben. "Well, she's certainly pretty," the older woman teased. "I can see why you want her working with you this summer."

Molly's eyes grew wide, and Ben flushed.

"Th-th-that's not why," he stammered. "I mean, she's my sister's friend. As I said, she's friendly, outgoing, well organized, and a hard worker."

"All the things you're not, huh?" Pat Abbott said, raising her eyebrows. "Then, tell me, Ben, why did I hire you?"

He grinned and said, "OK, I *do* work hard. And I have lots of imagination. And you want to give me a chance to see if I have what it takes to be a full-time do-gooder like you."

"That's why I hired you? And all this time I thought it was just because you were cute," Mrs. Abbott teased.

*Cute?* Molly glanced several times back and forth from Ben to Mrs. Abbott. *Ben Jackson, cute?* His nose was straight, and his skin was smooth. His eyes were his best feature, expressive and dark. She decided he *was* cute, in an older-brother way.

Pat Abbott turned and focused her full attention on Molly. "So, why do you want to work with kids?" she asked.

"I don't know that I do. That is, I want to do something worthwhile this summer, and Ben suggested that I talk to you about the summer program," Molly said. That was the truth.

"Have you had experience working with kids?"

"None at all. But I'm willing to learn. I've taken art every year in school, and I was a Girl Scout, so I think I could help with crafts and art projects. And I can play the guitar some, if that helps," Molly replied.

Mrs. Abbott seemed pleased. "That all sounds terrific. Ben says you're well organized. What did he mean by that?"

Molly was silent for a moment. Then she

said, "I'm not sure. I've been active in school clubs and projects, and we've always managed to get the job done. I guess if I can get the school administrators to cooperate with me, maybe I could get the little kids to cooperate, too."

"Do you think you'd like to take up this kind of work permanently when you're out of school?" Mrs. Abbott asked.

"I don't know," Molly answered honestly. "I've never thought about it. Who knows, I might love working with kids and end up majoring in child psychology. Think of me as another recruit for the cause."

Mrs. Abbott laughed heartily. "Take this application form home, Molly, and fill it out. There's a place on there for your parents to sign. It's required for anyone under eighteen. You can drop it off here tomorrow evening, but as far as I'm concerned, the job is yours if you want it."

"You mean it?" Molly was thrilled. She hadn't been sure until just then that she really wanted the job. It was great to think she'd be working for someone as likable as Pat Abbott.

"I mean it. I like your honesty. I've turned down several people for this job because they kept telling me how they had always wanted to work with underprivileged kids. I didn't buy it. All they wanted to do was nail down a steady job. Oh, by the way, you do know that you won't get rich at this."

Molly snapped her fingers. "Darn! Ben said we'd start at twenty dollars an hour."

Ben looked worried. "Molly, don't do that to me. She'll believe you."

"Don't worry, Ben," Pat said. "If anyone makes twenty bucks an hour, it had better be me since I'm the director."

"Well, we'd better be going," Ben said. "Thanks, Pat. You won't regret hiring Molly. I'll keep her in line. It's a job I'm used to. This girl has hung around my house for years."

"And who's going to keep you in line, Ben?" Molly asked. "Keeping track of kids I can manage, but I think disciplining you is beyond my powers."

Molly and Ben said goodbye to Pat and went out to the car. The ride back to Skip's, where Molly's car was parked, was silent; Ben concentrated on driving, while Molly was lost in thought. So much had happened to her in twenty-four hours.

Ben pulled up next to Molly's car and waited for her to get out. Molly stared at the defective door in dismay, waiting for Ben to let her out on his side.

After they had sat there in silence for a few

40

seconds, Ben said, "I know I'm great company, Mol. But since we'll be spending a lot of time together this summer, do you think you could bring yourself to hop out? This car guzzles gas when it's idling."

"Ben, I *can't* get out. And it has nothing to do with how irresistible you are, believe me. This door can't be opened from the inside, remember? At Mrs. Abbott's I crawled out from your side, but that's impossible at the moment since you're sitting there," Molly said.

"Oops, sorry," Ben said. He put the car in neutral, pulled on the emergency brake, and got out. Molly waited for him to come around and open her door. Instead, he stood on the driver's side, waiting for her to slide across the seat.

"Thanks. You're a real gentleman," Molly mumbled sarcastically as she stepped out of the car.

"Anytime," he replied. "See you at the park."

"Right, Ben," Molly answered.

As she climbed into her shiny little car, Molly wondered what she had gotten herself into. After all her talk about doing something worthwhile, she could now look forward to spending the entire summer working with a bunch of little kids and Ben Jackson.

# Chapter Five

The last week of school flashed by in a blur for Molly. She and Kristi studied for all their tests together, and Molly knew she'd done well. The prospect of working five days a week all summer long hung over her like a shadow, especially when she would listen to the other kids' plans to go to the beach or rafting. But then she'd run into Robert and Linda in the hallway, and her resolve would harden again; she would work as hard as she could all summer, knowing that for once she was really doing something important.

Other than Robert and Linda's romance, which was the talk of the school, there was another reason Molly couldn't wait for school to be out and her job to start—the bet. Everyone teased her about it mercilessly. Molly suddenly realized that she had never really been without a boy, Robert or someone else, by her side. It bugged her that people thought she was incapable of being by herself. *Well*, Molly thought, *I'll see them all back here next fall—with Kristi as my slave!*

Molly woke up early the first day of work. She showered and put her blond hair into a tight french braid, then slipped into a white tank top and pleated khaki shorts. She grabbed the lunch she'd packed the night before and drove over to the park. She arrived fifteen minutes early, so she got out of her car and leaned against it, waiting for the others to come.

Soon everyone was assembled, and Pat introduced them all. The student crew included Molly, Ben, another Oak Park High School student, Paul Griffin, Alicia Martin, who was from St. Paul Academy, and an exchange student named Ingrid Holstrom, who was living with Alicia for the year. The other adult worker was an ex-nurse named Millie Sinclair.

Pat Abbott was dressed in jogging clothes and wore an impressive-looking silver whistle around her neck. She gathered them together around a wooden picnic table and went over the day's activities. She had just finished when the kids started arriving.

Molly watched with astonishment. They came in droves, in all shapes and sizes, all bearing paper lunch bags or colorful lunch boxes. Some kids came alone, others were in pairs, some were on foot, others were dropped off. Some looked eager, some seemed hesitant, some looked just plain scared.

"I've never seen anything like it," Molly whispered to Ben. "Were they expecting this many?"

He shrugged. Molly noticed that he had "dressed up" for his first day on the job. His shirt was tucked neatly into his jeans, and he had gotten a haircut.

"Ben, what are we going to *do* with them all?" Molly asked.

Some of the kids stood around as if they were waiting for instructions, while others took off in all directions to swing, slide, climb on the jungle gym, or tumble in the grass.

"Oh, it'll turn out," he said casually. "Pat told me to expect this."

Molly gave up on him and turned to observe the reactions of her coworkers. Ingrid was staring at a group of kids who were swinging;

Paul was laughing as he watched the kids scrambling around; Alicia remained cool and aloof, carefully inspecting her coral pink nails; Millie Sinclair seemed to be taking stock of the situation; and Pat, who had been through this many times before, looked amused.

At precisely eight o'clock, Pat looked down at her watch, took a deep breath, and raised the whistle to her lips. The shrill sound pierced the air; the kids stopped in their tracks.

"Everyone come over here," Pat boomed out. Molly was impressed.

"For those of you who don't remember me from last summer, or who are here for the first time, I'm Pat, and these are my assistants."

One by one, she introduced the rest of the crew.

"We're here to have a good time," Pat said. "And to learn things. But we have to obey the rules, or we're in trouble. Anyone here who can't obey rules?"

No one answered. The kids looked ready to behave, and Molly's fears faded. At least the summer wasn't going to be boring. With so many kids to look after, there wouldn't be a dull moment.

"If you don't mind us, you don't come back.

That's not just a rule; that's the law," Pat added for emphasis.

The younger kids looked impressed. Molly was in awe. Pat spoke with authority without sounding bossy or unpleasant.

"First thing we do is take our lunches and put them on the table over there. Does everyone have his or her name on their lunch?" Pat asked the children. Most of them nodded. Ben and Paul helped the rest by providing pens.

The next step was to divide the children into age groups.

"You take this group, Molly," Pat directed, pointing to a group of ten seven-to-nine-year-olds.

Within a few minutes order had been created. Molly found herself confronted with ten expectant faces.

"Shouldn't there have been a training session for this?" Molly called to Ben who was at the next table. His kids were older than the ones in Molly's group.

"You need *training* to string and paste shells?" he called back.

*No*, Molly muttered to herself. That wasn't exactly what she had meant. Shells she could handle; it was the kids she was worried about. *Calm down*, she told herself. *Just be yourself and wing it.*

"All of you know my name is Molly. But I don't know any of your names, so you're going to have to help me out," Molly said.

"I'm Peter," one boy volunteered.

"My name is Jennifer," a small girl piped up. Other kids shouted their names.

"Wait a minute," Molly said, holding her hands to her ears and squeezing her eyes shut for a moment. "I can't hear any of you if you all talk at once!" She smiled at them. They giggled and settled down.

"We'll use a game to help me remember your names, OK?" Everyone nodded. "My name is Molly, and I like something that starts with the same letter as my name. My name is Molly, and I like movies." She pointed to the boy next to her. "Now you tell me who you are."

"My name is Peter, and I like Popsicles," he said.

"And who am I?" Molly asked him.

"Your name is Molly, and you like movies," he answered. Molly nodded.

"Now you," Molly said, pointing to the girl next to Peter.

"My name is Danielle, and I like dancing!" she said enthusiastically. "He is Peter, and he likes Popsicles, and you are Molly, and you like movies!"

"Terrific!" Molly said. The game was going

well. As they went around the circle and the list got longer, the kids, amid much laughter, would help one another out.

Finally it was one of the youngest girls' turns to give her name and repeat the game. But she would only stare at her lap, her brown hair falling over her face.

"What's your name?" Molly asked encouragingly.

"She's Robin," Danielle answered. "She never talks."

"Robin?" Molly said gently. "Can you tell me what you like?"

The small girl sat silently, unmoved by the tone in Molly's voice.

"That's OK," Molly said, trying to hurry the game along. "We're all a little shy at first. Would anyone like to start pasting shells on boxes?"

The kids nodded and ran over to the table on which the supplies were laid out. Molly supervised their projects carefully, letting the kids who wanted help ask her for it and leaving the others to work on their own. Slowly she started to relax. As she looked over the table of busy hands and intent faces, she realized that she was having fun.

She walked over to where Robin was sitting. The little girl was carefully gluing shells onto a cigar box. Her fingers were nimble and sure as she arranged the shells into a star pattern.

"It's very good," Molly said softly. She didn't want to praise any one child too much, but she wanted to let Robin know that her project was well done.

Molly's words had the opposite effect of what she had intended. Robin's hands froze, and she didn't touch the box again until Molly had moved on. Had she hurt Robin's feelings? Molly wondered. *Give her time*, Molly told herself.

Arts and crafts, Molly soon discovered, was the easy part of the day. Trying to keep up with her crew during the games and exercises made her feel like an old woman. Molly had always considered herself fairly athletic, but her kids' abilities were much better than hers. And they never tired. They didn't even get winded. The sandwich Molly brought for lunch only made a small dent in her hunger, and she made a mental note to pack a bigger lunch the next day.

The afternoon passed quickly. Toward the end of the day, Molly led her kids in singing. She liked being surrounded by the group as they sang energetically. Then she noticed Robin, who was sitting away from the other kids, her small face tense and angry. Molly was at a loss. Why did Robin seem so unhappy?

Finally it was three o'clock, and the children began to depart almost as rapidly as they had arrived.

"You guys can go," Pat told the counselors when only a few stragglers remained. "It's always like this. Some parents are late picking them up. Thanks for a terrific first day. This just might be the best summer program yet."

Molly felt encouraged by Pat's praise. She had just started toward her car when she heard Ben call, "Wait up a minute, Molly."

Molly glanced toward the shelter house, where Ben stood with two little kids. Molly smiled to herself. She wondered if Ben still wanted to spend his life working with children or if one day had been enough.

The small boys, obviously brothers, were listening raptly to Ben. Molly watched as Ben gestured, waving them over to a table to point something out. Just then a car pulled up, and its driver, a young man, called to the boys. They left Ben in midsentence.

"We'll continue tomorrow, sports," he called.

"You won't forget about the ocean, Ben?" one boy yelled back.

"I won't forget."

51

"What about the ocean?" Molly teased.

"Oh, I have some examples of saltwater shells at home. I promised Jason and Justin I'd bring them. They're sharp little kids, really interested in science, I think," Ben commented.

His face was relaxed and happy. Ben had survived the first day in great shape.

"How did it go with you?" he asked. "I wanted to catch you before you left."

"OK, once I got over my initial panic," she said. Molly always liked to appear to be in control of a situation, but for some reason, she didn't mind Ben knowing that she had been scared.

"You looked a bit uncertain there for a while," he said.

"That's the way I felt. But, for the most part, I enjoyed it. I really did," she told him. They started to walk toward the parking lot.

They both spotted Robin in the same moment. She was sitting alone on a large flat rock, and tears were rolling down her face.

"What's the matter there, I wonder?" Ben asked. He and Molly started toward her.

Molly sighed. "That's Robin. She's my biggest failure of the day. She's shy or something. And I can't get her to talk. I tried off and on all day. Either she won't look at me, or she glares at me. She doesn't seem to like me at all."

"Don't be silly," Ben said, laughing softly. "She's just a little kid. You suppose someone's forgotten to pick her up?"

Molly shrugged. Ben walked over to where Robin was sitting.

"Your shoes are untied," he announced. Robin didn't move.

"Want me to tie them for you?" Ben asked. The little girl still didn't answer.

"Well, all right, since you've begged me, I'll tie them. But just this once," he said. Ben knelt in front of Robin and tied her shoe laces. But he tied the strings of her right shoe to the strings of the left one.

"Someone coming to pick you up pretty soon?" he asked.

Robin nodded, staring down at her shoes. Her tears had stopped.

"Great. When your ride gets here, you'll be all ready to go," Ben told her.

A small giggle escaped Robin as she seemed to realize she couldn't go anywhere.

"That's more like it," Ben said. "If you're sad, I'm sad. If you're happy, I'm happy."

A beige car was coming down the road, and Robin looked at it anxiously.

"Yours?" Ben asked.

Robin nodded.

"Then hop up," he ordered.

"I can't." Her first words were spoken in a voice that was barely audible.

"Why not?" he asked with mock severity.

She pointed down to where her shoes were tied to each other.

Ben bent down and untied the knot he had made. "Now what? We're back where we started, aren't we?"

Robin looked directly at Ben and smiled hesitantly. Then she squatted down and tied her own shoes. "Hey, you're a real pro at that," Ben said.

"I've done it since I was five," Robin told him. "I'm seven."

"Terrific. Well, see you tomorrow, Robin," Ben said.

She waved at him and walked toward the car.

Molly joined in. She called out, "Think up a song you'd like to sing tomorrow, Robin. I'll let you pick the first one if you like."

Molly saw Robin's shoulders tense up. The little girl moved stiffly over to the car and climbed in. She didn't look back.

Molly felt defeated. "You said you were going to get pointers from me," Molly told Ben. "I think I'm the one who needs to take lessons from you."

He patted her on the back. "Don't worry about it, Mol. I'm doing better than I thought I would, but I have to work at it, too. Robin is just a kid who needs time to get to know people. I bet you'll win her over before the summer's over."

"I hope so," Molly said.

"Speaking of bets," Ben said slowly. "How's your bet with Kristi coming along?" His gray eyes were serious, although the tone of his voice was light and friendly.

"Oh, that," Molly said. Ben couldn't know about the teasing she'd gotten the last week of school. "I mean, I'm here, aren't I?"

"You know, Molly, you don't have to be extreme about this," Ben told her. "You can be a 'worthwhile' person, to use your word, and still date."

Molly stared at him. "Are you kidding? I have my reputation to uphold. The whole school knows that Kristi and I have our bet, and I'm going to win it. And, anyway," she added, "if today is any indication of what we can expect this summer, I'm going to be too tired after work to think, let alone go out on a date."

"OK, Molly, anything you say," Ben said, his

eyes twinkling. "There must be a lot of guys in Oak Park wondering if they'll be the one to make you lose that bet."

"Well, they can just keep on wondering," Molly snapped. "I've made a decision, and I'm sticking by it."

Ben touched her shoulder as they stood by Molly's car. "Molly, don't get so mad. Remember me? I'm on your side—much to Kristi's dismay."

Molly glanced at his hand on her shoulder, which he quickly dropped to his side. His shirt had come untucked, his jeans had dirt ground into the knees, and his unruly hair was curlier than usual in the humidity. Molly realized that Ben really was the only person she knew who wasn't waiting for her to fall on her face. She smiled at him.

"Thanks, Ben," she said simply.

"You're welcome, Molly," Ben replied.

"I'd better get going," Molly said, climbing into the front seat of her car and rolling down the window.

"See you tomorrow," Ben said.

"Only four days until the weekend," Molly called, backing out of her parking spot. "I'm just kidding," she said in answer to Ben's perplexed look. "I'm actually looking forward to tomorrow." She waved and drove off.

On the way home Molly remembered the tender way Ben had looked at Robin. He'd had that same look on his face when he was telling her that he was on her side.

*Ben Jackson*, she thought. *Defender of animals, small children, and me.*

# Chapter Six

Molly and a group of children sat cross-legged on the ground on Friday. She strummed the guitar to the last strains of "Froggie Went A-Courtin'." She had taught it to them a few days earlier.

"Let's sing it one more time," Jennifer begged.

"And I get to make the chords this time," Brian said insistently.

Molly sighed. She was going to have to dig up other verses to the song, for a little variety.

"Please, Molly?" Jennifer pleaded.

Molly looked at the shining faces and hopeful eyes and gave in. "This is the fourth and last time," she said firmly.

She showed Brian where to put his fingers

to make the chord when she indicated it was time. " 'Froggie went a courtin', He did ride, Sword and pistol by his side,' " she sang, and nine other voices sang along with her.

When the song was over, Molly started to take the guitar strap from around the neck.

"You sing by yourself, Molly," Megan demanded. "You promised on Monday you'd sing this week."

Molly had hoped that they would forget her promise. She wasn't very confident about being the center of attention, even for a group of kids.

"Yes, but we're out of time," she said, hedging.

Mark said, "Not until Alicia calls us over."

"All right," Molly agreed reluctantly, feeling suddenly shy.

"You can pick the song," Megan said graciously.

"We'll hum along," David piped up.

"Here's one my daddy sang to me when I was your age," Molly said.

Self-consciously she began to sing "The Bear Went Over the Mountain." The kids were such an attentive audience that she soon forgot her fears. Her voice grew stronger and more sure. The words were simple and repetitive. In no time at all, the group was singing the lively tune along with her.

"Hey, look at Robin," Megan said when the song was over. "It made her cry. I thought it was a funny song."

Molly glanced over at the little girl who steadfastly refused to talk to her.

"I'm not crying over that dumb song," Robin said angrily. "*She* can't sing so good anyway. My mother can sing a lot better than *she* can." The child's whole body trembled.

The entire group turned toward Robin. It was the longest speech she had ever uttered, and the others were fascinated.

Robin looked up at Molly and for the first time spoke to her directly. "You're not so great. You think you can sing, but you can't. You think you're pretty, but you're not. You're just an old ugly girl, and I hate you!"

The other children watched Molly, too shocked to speak.

Molly was hurt and angry, but she was determined not to let her feelings show.

"I'm sorry you feel that way, Robin. I only sang because the others wanted me to. It's fun to sing even if you don't have a terrific voice. And try not to hold the way I look against me. I didn't get to pick out my face, you know.

61

"Now, run along," she ordered. "Alicia's waiting for all of you."

The ten youngsters got up and ran toward Alicia. Amy was almost all the way there when she turned around and ran back to Molly. Flinging her small arms around Molly's neck, she kissed her on the cheek and whispered, "You sing pretty, and you look pretty, Molly." Then she ran back to join the others without giving Molly a chance to speak.

Molly sank down on the grass and leaned back against a tree. Robin's outburst was unreasonable, but Molly didn't know what to do. The feel of the solid trunk behind her was comforting.

She watched Alicia, slender and supple, leading the children in aerobics exercises. Molly suppressed a twinge of envy. Alicia's long, dark hair moved like a velvet curtain. She was so elegantly thin and graceful that she made Molly feel like a blimp in comparison.

"Taking it easy?" Ben asked, sauntering over to the tree where Molly sat. He plopped down beside her.

"You might say that," she replied. "I have a few free moments before I have to go pour juice and hand out cookies for break time. I've just been watching Alicia. She's certainly good, isn't she?"

Ben looked toward Alicia.

"Yes," he said after long contemplation. "She's good." Molly thought his eyes had a glazed look to them. Could Ben have a crush on Alicia? Everything about her was perfect: her face, her hair, her figure. Even her fingernails were perfect—beautifully manicured and polished.

"She's awfully pretty, too, don't you think?" Molly asked.

Ben looked at her, his expression unreadable. He shrugged and said, "I guess so."

"Is she in your class at St. Paul?" Molly asked.

Ben nodded. "I don't see much of her. I take science electives, and she's concentrating on performing arts. I stay away from that stuff."

"Why?" Molly teased. "You'd look cute in a leotard."

Ben slugged her lightly on the arm. "By the way, how's the job going?"

"I like it," Molly admitted. "More than I thought I would. But I wish I could iron out my problems with Robin. She hates me, and I don't know why. I don't expect everyone to adore me. But I can't understand why she dislikes me so much. Maybe I should ask Pat to put her in a different group."

Ben reached out and placed a hand on her

shoulder. It felt brotherly and reassuring. "You're sure you're not making something out of nothing?" he asked softly. "You know, making things out to be worse than they really are?"

"I wish I could believe that," she said bitterly. Molly told him about Robin's outburst.

He let out a low whistle when she had finished.

"That is weird," Ben said.

"Tell me about it," Molly answered sadly.

Ben placed a fingertip under her chin and tilted her face toward his. Molly tried to blink back the tears in her eyes.

"The little kid has a problem," he told her gently. "We have no way of knowing what it is. But none of it is *your* fault, Molly. I've heard you singing with the kids, and you're pretty good. And you're most certainly not 'an old ugly girl.' "

"You trying to give me a compliment, Ben Jackson?" Molly asked, struggling to smile.

"Sort of, I guess. I'm not very good at that sort of thing."

"You could tell me I'm insanely beautiful," she said.

He gave her a lopsided grin. "I could, couldn't I? But I didn't. You look OK to me, Molly."

Molly wiped her arm across her eyes. "You know, Ben," she said thoughtfully, "I never did back down from a challenge. And Robin is certainly a challenge. If only I knew what's bugging her, maybe I could help. No little kid should run around as tense as she is."

"It's worth a try. It certainly couldn't hurt," Ben agreed.

Molly jumped to her feet, feeling the adrenaline rise with her enthusiasm. "Then you'll help me?"

"Help you? With what?" Ben sounded wary.

"Find out about Robin. You know, do a little detective work. We could follow her home in my car and then hang around and see what goes on there."

"What do you want us to do, stake out Robin's house?" Ben asked, shaking his head in disbelief. "This isn't a TV detective show, Molly. This is real life. If we hang around some strange place and nose around, we're likely to get the cops called on us."

"Don't be silly," Molly said, giving him a withering look. "We're going to use common sense. All we're going to do is see where she lives and what kind of family she has."

Ben rubbed his eyes. "Molly, be realistic. What can you tell me about the members of

Robin's family from what you see in a car parked across the street?"

"We have to start somewhere. It seems as good a place as any to me. What's gotten into you? You've always been the white knight, the big crusader. Now I want to do something to help that sad little girl, and you're dragging your feet." Molly's tone was accusing.

Ben's voice was very quiet when he spoke. "Are you really concerned about Robin, Molly? Or is it your bruised ego that's bothering you?"

She was instantly indignant. "What do you mean by that?"

"Don't get hostile, Molly. I know you're used to being Miss Popularity. Most of us come across people like Robin all the time—people who obviously don't like us and don't want anything to do with us. Maybe they even make fun of us, and we don't know why. It hurts, sure, but there's not a lot we can do about it. You have a whole bunch of kids who are crazy about you. Think about the successes and don't dwell on the one failure."

"Ben Jackson, I think you're just awful! I really do. My motives in this aren't as selfish as you think. Anyone in this whole, wide world has the right to hate me—and, for that matter, I've probably run across more back stabbers than you seem to think," Molly said. "But whether you believe me or not, it's Robin I'm thinking about. She doesn't really relate to the other kids. I've never seen her try to make friends. She never smiles; she won't sing; and she always finds some excuse to hang back and not do the dances and gymnastics. Even when we do crafts, she just seems to go through the motions like a robot. You told me lots of troubled, neglected kids came to this camp. Well, in my opinion, Robin's about the most troubled one here. Are you going to stand there, Mr. Future Guidance Counselor, and tell me you don't think Robin needs some special help?" she demanded.

Ben's nod was barely perceptible. He did not comment on her tirade. All he did was squint at her in the sunlight and say, "OK. You want to start this on Monday?"

"Does that mean you're willing to help?" Molly asked.

"Yes," Ben said.

"Then Monday it is!" Molly said triumphantly.

# Chapter Seven

Molly cherished her weekend. She liked her work; she loved the children. But five days in a row were enough. By the time Friday afternoon rolled around, Molly was ready to relax.

Saturday afternoon Molly decided to spend some of her hard-earned money on a shopping spree at the mall. She parked near the boutique where Kristi worked. Inside the store Molly looked around for Kristi, but she wasn't there. The store manager, recognizing Molly from the other times she'd been in to visit, told her that Kristi was on her break. Then Kristi breezed in, noisily sipping the last bit of a Diet Pepsi.

"Molly!" she cried. "If I'd known you were coming, I would have saved my break."

"That's all right," Molly replied. "I'm supposed to be doing some shopping, but nothing seems to appeal to me."

"If you need summer dresses, we have some really cute ones," Kristi said, leading her over to a rack against the wall.

"Actually, I just got here," Molly admitted. "I thought I was in the mood to shop, but now that I'm here, I don't really need anything."

"Since when did we shop because we needed things?" Kristi asked her. "You'd look great in one of these," she added, holding up an ice-blue sun dress to Molly.

Molly surveyed herself in the mirror. "Is this dress fingerprint and mudpie proof?" she asked.

"What?" Kristi asked. "Oh—I forgot. You're interested in our superpractical baby-sitter's line of sportswear."

"Kristi, I'm not exactly a baby-sitter—I'm called a park counselor," Molly said, pretending to be angry with her friend.

"Sorry," Kristi said. "I just thought this sun dress might help my chances of winning the bet."

"I'll win the bet," Molly said. "No matter what I happen to be wearing."

"Well, all I know is that while I was on my break at the Gingerbread House, I saw Robert

Prentiss lurking around with Joe Larson. If you ask me, he was just about to come up and ask me about you."

"What happened?" Molly asked casually.

"Oh, you are interested?" Kristi said. "Well, nothing happened. I got up and came back here. My break was over."

Molly put the dress back on the rack. "I should let you get back to work, then. What time are you off?"

"Eight—when the mall closes. Will you be around tonight?"

"I think I'm going to read magazines and soak in the tub," Molly answered. "I'm still beat from this past week."

"Name: Molly Kincaid. Occupation: recluse," Kristi accused.

"That's not true," Molly said. "Let's have a pizza tomorrow night, all right?"

"I'm always up for a pizza," Kristi said. "Oops, the boss is giving me the eye. Have fun shopping, and I'll talk to you tomorrow."

Molly waved and walked out into the brick-lined mall. The urge to shop had vanished. She decided to wander around, look in a few windows, and waste some time. That, to her, would be a luxury.

An hour later Molly felt thirsty and tired.

71

She had tried on some clothes but couldn't get into it.

She slid onto one of the stools at the Gingerbread House counter and ordered a chocolate milkshake. When it came, she toyed with it, watching other shoppers around the courtyard. During the week it was easy to forget that the whole world wasn't under age ten.

Then her gaze landed on the fair head of Robert Prentiss. He was looking at her from across the mall. Molly cast her eyes down while she sipped her milkshake. When she glanced up again, Robert's back was to her, but his friend, Joe Larson, was staring right at her. Molly knew, without a doubt, that they were discussing her.

Molly's heart started to pound. She didn't want to talk to Robert, but if he came over to the Gingerbread House, she wouldn't be able to avoid it. She didn't want that.

Molly dug around in her purse for money to pay for the milkshake. Then she dashed out one of the side doors of the mall, without once looking back.

*Darn*, thought Molly. *Why does Robert make me react like that?* Most days she didn't have time to think about Robert. On one of her only days off, she had run into him. It wasn't fair.

*   *   *

The telephone rang that evening, and Molly's mother answered it. When she told Molly that a boy wanted to talk to her, Molly's heart almost skipped a beat. She knew it was Robert. Seeing him at the mall had stirred up all kinds of old feelings. Maybe Robert felt the same way. They had once had fun together. If she accepted just *one* date on a trial basis, that didn't mean they had to start going together again exclusively.

Slowly Molly made her way toward the telephone. She had made up her mind to go out with him if he asked her. Then images of Kristi, her parents, Ben, and all the other people who knew about her vow not to date popped to the surface. The bet! If she did go out with Robert on a trial basis, she would lose the bet with Kristi. *Well*, she decided, *Robert isn't worth that. Not after the way he treated me.*

She picked up the receiver. "Hello?"

"Uh, Molly, this is Joe Larson. I know it's short notice, but I was wondering if you'd be free to go roller-skating tonight."

Molly was speechless for a moment. "I'm sorry, Joe," she managed to say at last. "It's nothing personal, but I just don't date anymore."

"Yeah, well, I heard that. I wasn't sure if it was true or not. I figured it wouldn't hurt to try," he said.

"Thanks for asking me," she said warmly. "I do appreciate it."

"Sure. And if you change your mind, put out the word."

"I'll do that," Molly said.

After hanging up the phone, she went to her room and flopped down on the bed. Joe was nice, but she wasn't willing to lose the bet for him.

*What about Robert?* she asked herself.

Molly knew that she wasn't still hung up on Robert. Things could never be the same between them again. And he had taught her a lesson, a lesson she had learned well. *All* boys were more trouble than they were worth. She had no intention of getting involved with one again.

Sunday afternoon stretched out long and lazily. Molly grew restless and called Kristi to see if she was still interested in going out for a pizza.

"Can you pick me up?" Kristi asked. "My parents took their car, and that other monstrosity isn't running. It made a funny noise yesterday and hasn't been the same since. I think it died. Ben's out working on it now, but I don't think he's getting anywhere. I told him he was wasting his time, and now he isn't speaking to me."

Molly laughed. "I'll be there in fifteen minutes or so."

When she pulled up in front of Kristi's house, the first thing she saw was Ben's long legs sticking out from under the battered vehicle.

"Hi, Ben," she called cheerfully.

"Hello, Molly," Ben answered. His words sounded muffled.

"What's the trouble?" Molly asked.

"I don't know. That's what I'm trying to find out. She's got an awful rattle in her—kind of like a cough," Ben said.

"Maybe it's terminal," Molly suggested.

He poked his head out long enough to give her a distinctly dirty look. His clothes were covered in grease and dirt, and a black smudge covered the side of his nose. "Don't start. I hear enough of that from my sweet little sister. What are you doing here, anyway?"

Molly smiled sweetly. "Thanks for making me feel welcome at your home, Ben."

He shrugged. "You're welcome enough. I just asked why you were here. I didn't figure you dropped by just to see me. Insulting my

75

car may be great sport, but it's hardly worth a trip from your house."

"Kristi and I are going to get a pizza."

"Pizza, huh?" Ben said.

Molly felt torn. Ben had really perked up at the mention of pizza. Molly knew that she should ask him if he wanted to join them, but she didn't want to ask. She was looking forward to spending time with Kristi. Seeing Ben five days a week was enough.

Just then Kristi came running out of the house. "Hi, Molly. Hope I didn't keep you waiting. Pizza! I guess I really should just have a salad, though. These jeans get tighter every time I wear them." She tugged at the waistband. "Oh, well," she said with a sigh. "I can always start my diet tomorrow."

"Are you going to bring me some?" Ben asked.

Molly felt relieved. Apparently Ben wasn't even thinking about going with them.

"I don't know," Kristi said slowly. "You got any money? Molly and I generally split a medium, and there's usually not much left. More pizza costs more money, you know."

Ben took out his wallet. Handing her three dollars, he said, "Bring me back a few slices."

Molly swallowed hard and let her good manners win out. "You could come with us, Ben," she suggested. "I mean, if you want hot pizza."

Ben glanced up at her. He looked startled. "You mean that? You're actually asking me to come with you?"

He sounded so surprised that Molly felt ashamed of her earlier reluctance.

"Why not?" Molly asked.

"Good grief, Ben," Kristi said, sounding exasperated. "Are you coming or not?"

Ben's eyes were riveted on Molly as if he were trying to read her thoughts. Molly stared back, not really sure if she wanted him along or not. After a long silence, he said quietly, "Thanks for asking, but just go ahead and bring me some when you're through. I don't mind cold pizza. I need to get this car running by the morning, and I don't want to take the time to wash up. Don't pig out too much."

Molly felt a little disappointed. She knew that Ben had sensed he wasn't wanted. She tried to make it up to him.

"I don't mean to sound as if I don't have confidence in your mechanical ability," she said. "But if, by some chance, you don't get that car running by the morning, give me a call. I'll come pick you up. All right?"

Ben smiled broadly, and Molly felt relief flood her. He wasn't mad at her.

77

"Thanks, Molly," he said. "I may have to take you up on that."

"It'll hurt my feelings if I get to the park and find you've walked there. See you later," Molly said. He waved.

"It must be great to be an only child," Kristi said, once they were heading for the pizza place. "Ben and I are so close in age that our folks can't possibly afford to buy cars for each of us, not with Ben in private school and both of us going to college in a couple of years."

"I guess that's an advantage to being an only child," Molly said. "But I'm not sure the advantages aren't outweighed by the disadvantages. I always feel as though I'm missing out on a lot. I really envy big families."

"You wouldn't want a brother like Ben," Kristi said. "You can't imagine what it's like having him around."

"Oh, I don't know," Molly replied thoughtfully. "Ben's different from a lot of guys. We get along OK at the park. Of course, we're usually working at different things at different times. But he's really a pretty nice person."

"Nice? I didn't say he wasn't nice. But I think he's the only male in Oak Park who plays Scrabble during the Super Bowl."

"To each his own," Molly said with a laugh. She preferred Scrabble to football, too.

Kristi told her, "He says, 'If you've seen one football game, you've seen them all.' "

Molly agreed with Ben.

They had already placed their order when Robert Prentiss came in with a girl and sat down in a booth across the room. Molly wondered if running into him was her destiny that weekend.

"Want to leave?" Kristi said in a whisper.

Molly did, but she wasn't about to say so. "No, it's OK," she said with deliberate casualness. "We've already ordered. And I got over Robert ages ago."

"Looks as if he's gotten rid of Linda already," Kristi whispered.

"So I noticed. But I can't understand why he'd replace Linda with Peggy Summers. Linda's awfully pretty, but Peggy—"

"She's nice," Kristi interrupted. "I didn't think she was very friendly at first, but I worked with her on a dance committee last year. When you get to know her, she has a great sense of humor."

"Oh, well, it doesn't matter," Molly said, doing her best to look bored.

Kristi knew her too well to be fooled. "I can read you, Molly. So I hope you can stand a little advice, because I feel some coming on. If you still want him, go after him."

"Not on your life! Where did you get the idea that I was still interested in Robert?" Molly asked.

Kristi looked down at the tabletop, a grin spreading across her face. For the first time ever, Molly could see some resemblance between Kristi and her brother.

"OK, Kris, what's the joke? Tell me and we can both laugh," Molly said.

"I'm sorry if I'm irritating you. I guess I just caught on to something. It always takes me awhile to get a point. OK, I believe you when you say you don't care anything about Robert."

"Great. Now all I have to do is convince the rest of the world," Molly grumbled.

"See, that's it," Kristi said triumphantly. "What's bugging you is your pride. You're going around all worried about what everyone is thinking. You think if Robert's replacing you, he should pick perfect girls, not ordinary ones like Peggy."

Molly was both hurt and angry. How could Kristi talk to her like that? Best friends were supposed to be sympathetic. Molly couldn't think of a retort. The two girls sat across from each other in awkward silence. Just as the silence began to seem unbearable, the pizza arrived.

"It's great pizza," commented Molly as she bit into a slice.

"You said it!" Kristi agreed. She relaxed. "And this is my favorite kind. I just may forget to save some for Ben."

"Better not," Molly advised. "After taking his money, you're likely to get your nose twisted off with his wrench."

"I'm not worried. Knowing my brother's mechanical ability, I could escape before he figured out how to use it."

Molly laughed. "Look, Kris," she said, "I'm sorry I got mad. You're right, Robert Prentiss is a sore subject with me. It was a new experience, getting rejected like that. My pride's been bent out of shape ever since Robert and I broke up. But I predict I'll survive."

"Definitely. And look at it this way: at least you had something good together for a little while," Kristi said. "I haven't. Right now, I'm crazy about Sean Gray. He's working at the stereo outlet at the mall. I've learned a lot about stereos on my lunch hours."

"Getting anywhere?" Molly asked.

Sighing deeply, Kristi said, "If he knows I'm alive, he's keeping it a secret." She and Molly laughed.

"I'm stuffed," Molly announced. "How about you?"

Kristi nodded emphatically. "I couldn't hold another bite."

"Then it looks as if Ben gets the rest," Molly said.

While the waitress was putting the remainder of the pizza in a box for them, Molly bought a large soda.

"Still thirsty?" Kristi asked on the way out to the car.

Molly blushed. "I just thought Ben might want it to go with his pizza."

Kristi gave her a curious look and said, "His money's gone. I used it all to buy his share of the pizza."

"I know. Buying one soda won't break me. I just felt sorry for him, having to eat cold pizza and all. It's no big deal."

Kristi didn't say anything. But she did give Molly a long, studied look.

*About the last thing I need,* Molly thought, *is for Kristi to get the idea that I'm falling for Ben.* She and Ben were just working together! Molly was beginning to appreciate him as a person instead of seeing him simply as Kristi's big brother—that was all.

After dropping Kristi off, Molly thought about her weekend run-ins with Robert and her conversation with Kristi. Given time, Molly might actually thank Robert. His actions hadn't been pleasant, but they had introduced her to a simpler way of life—a way of life she planned to keep for a long, long time.

her conversation unaltered. Given that
. . . . with . . . a family plant-selling . . . . his
. . . . . before the . . . element but they had
. . . reduced her to the helpless ridicule . . . .
. . of life she planned to bring for a long, long
time.

# Chapter Eight

"Ben," Molly said first thing Monday morning, "I have to talk with you about Robin." Ben hadn't been able to get his car fixed, so Molly decided she'd make the most of the ride to work by discussing their plans.

"Right after Robin leaves today, we'll both get to my car as fast as we can," Molly began. "We'll follow her home at a distance, and we'll—"

"Wait a minute!" Ben said, laughing.

"Did I say something funny?" Molly asked.

"Not exactly," Ben answered. "But before we start sleuthing around, I think we should talk to Robin's mother when she comes to pick Robin up."

"But that's just the point, Ben! I don't think

that woman is Robin's mother. She hardly even glances at Robin when she gets into the car. Do you know any mother who wouldn't kiss her daughter after not seeing her all day?" Molly questioned.

"Well, then we should talk to that woman, whoever she is. Or we should talk to Pat. You can't just barge in on somebody's life, Molly," Ben said as they pulled into the parking lot.

Molly gazed over the hills behind the park. She didn't answer him.

"Molly, did you forget that all the kids' parents have filled out cards? We can find out a lot from Robin's card, if Pat will let us."

Molly sighed and climbed out of the car. "Your suggestions make more sense," she admitted. "But mine sound like more fun. I'm not too sure I want to start asking that woman questions. She doesn't look very friendly to me."

Ben laughed again. "You've got some imagination, Molly Kincaid! Do you think that woman in the beige car is going to whip out a gun when you tell her you're worried about Robin?"

Molly scowled and punched Ben lightly on the arm. "Go ahead, make fun of me. When she tells us to get lost and mind our own business, you'll be sorry."

Draping an arm casually around her shoulders, he said, "First let's go talk to Pat. Look, she just drove up."

Pat smiled at them. "Hello, early birds." Her expression became solemn as Molly and Ben explained their concern for Robin.

"With so many kids in the program," Pat said slowly, "I can't get to know all of them well. But meet me at the far picnic table after lunch, and I'll tell you the little I know about her."

After eating her sandwich and cookies, Molly found Ben, and they walked toward the picnic table where Pat was waiting.

"I don't have a lot to tell you," she said apologetically. "But maybe it's enough to help a little. Robin's parents are divorced, and Robin lives with her father. If she has any brothers or sisters, they don't come here. But I guess you knew that," Pat added.

"So how could we find out more?" Ben asked. "Molly's kind of developed a soft spot for Robin. I guess I have, too. We want to see what we can do to help."

"She needs a friend," Molly said eagerly. "I don't know why she's gotten to me the way she has. I can't explain it."

"I know, Molly. I get these feelings for the

kids myself. And I knew you would," Pat said. "That's why I hired you."

"And I thought it was my recommendation that did it," Ben quipped.

"Well, that, too," Pat replied. "I'll try to find out more about Robin and let you know."

"Do you think it would be OK to ask the woman who picks Robin up about her?" Molly asked.

"Let me check that out first," Pat said gently.

Molly felt relieved. She was glad that Pat had volunteered to talk to the woman. Still she hoped Pat would get back to her and Ben soon.

One evening a few days later, while listening to the stereo at Molly's house, Kristi said, "Gosh, you're all hyped up over this Robin thing, aren't you? You've just talked through two albums."

Molly grinned sheepishly. "Am I boring you? I guess I talk too much about it."

"I'm not bored," Kristi reassured her. "I'm just glad you're not moping around about Robert. Even if it means I'm going to lose our bet. I really didn't think you could make it all summer. It's all over town how you turned down Joe Larson."

Molly smiled to herself while Kristi talked. It was odd how much she had changed. The dating gossip just didn't seem important to her anymore.

"I'm glad I'm not moping, too. And I'm sure going to enjoy letting you do my homework next fall!"

Kristi made a face. "I can see I'm going to have to work on finding someone irresistible for you. And very soon."

"Just try," Molly challenged. "In the meantime, I'm happy."

Pat called Molly and Ben over to her during the lunch break the next Monday.

"I talked to Robin's father, and I talked to Mrs. Perkins, the woman who brings Robin to the park and picks her up every day," Pat told them. "I don't know if what I learned will be helpful or not. Robin's father seemed friendly and concerned. He says she's fine at home, talkative and affectionate with him. He and his wife were divorced about a year ago. They have another daughter several years younger than Robin. He took one child, and his wife took the other. His wife moved to California. Robin's only been out there once since the divorce. He says Robin didn't seem too upset at the time of the divorce and that she doesn't ever talk about it now."

"But if she doesn't *ever* talk about it, couldn't that be as big a problem as crying all the time or whatever?" Ben asked.

"Right," Pat said.

"What about Mrs. Perkins?" Molly asked eagerly.

"Not much help there," Pat told them. "She's not a relative or close family friend. She's someone who works with Robin's father. She has different hours, so Mr. James pays her to drive Robin. She didn't seem very concerned."

"I knew it!" Molly cried. Ben grinned at her.

"All the information I got from Mrs. Perkins," Pat said, "was that it was her opinion that Mr. James had spoiled the kid rotten and that Robin thinks she's too good to play with the other kids."

Molly shook her head. "I'm not buying that."

"Neither am I," Pat agreed. "We've had that kind here, and Robin doesn't fit the picture. But I don't think we can expect any help from Mrs. Perkins. I know it makes you feel helpless. But I think the important thing at this point is to keep showing Robin you care, and not to give up on her."

Pat left them alone then. Molly turned

toward Ben, and there was an excited look in her eyes.

"What now?" he asked suspiciously.

"I still think we should follow Robin home a few times, get to know her routine. It can't hurt. We might find out something helpful."

"And when do you want to start this?"

"What's the matter with today?" she suggested.

After Molly and Ben got off work, they sat in Molly's car, waiting for the familiar beige car to appear.

"This has to be one of the dumbest things I've ever done," Ben stated glumly.

"You don't *have* to be here, Ben. You're under no obligation to help."

"I'm not?" Ben asked.

"Look," Molly said. "If you're really skeptical about this and don't want to get involved, I'll understand. No hard feelings."

"But are you still going through with it?" Ben asked.

Molly shut her eyes for a minute and saw Robin's sad little face in her mind. No one that small should look so miserable all the time, she thought.

"I have to," she said quietly. "It may be dumb, but it's all I can think of right now. At least it makes me feel as though I'm doing something."

"Then count me in, too. Besides, I'm riding with you, remember? I guess I have to tag along with you. It's this or walk to work and back," Ben said.

Their conversation came to a halt when the beige car drove up, stopped at the spot where Robin waited alone, and then moved on when the little girl was safely inside. Molly felt a surge of excitement as she eased out of the parking place to follow the car.

"This is the first time I've ever tailed anyone," she announced happily.

"Can we hope it's also the last?"

"Let's see how it turns out. It may prove to be my true vocation in life. Molly Kincaid, Private Investigator. How does that sound?" she asked him.

"All right, I guess," he said.

Molly concentrated on keeping the beige car in sight.

"Relax!" Ben told Molly after he glanced over at her a few minutes later. Her spine was rigid, and she was leaning forward, her eyes riveted on the other car's back bumper.

"I guess I am uptight," she admitted, trying to loosen up. She sighed deeply and loosened her grip on the steering wheel. "I guess I need experience before I'm as cool as Sherlock Holmes."

"Is your aspiration to be like Sherlock Holmes?"

Molly didn't answer. The beige car took a sharp turn without signaling first, and she quickly followed.

"Do you think that woman knows we're following her? Do you think that's why she turned without signaling?" Molly asked anxiously.

"How would I know? Probably not. If she keeps doing it, then you can get worried," Ben said.

"Is it against the law to follow someone?" Molly asked.

Ben laughed heartily. "No, I don't see how it could be. Not unless they could prove harassment. Now will you calm down?"

Finally the driver of the beige car pulled up in front of a small house on Spring Street.

"Park here," Ben suggested. "See what happens."

Molly pulled over to the curb just before Robin's house and then shut off the engine. She peered anxiously out the windshield. Robin got out of the car and walked up the front walk toward the house without a backward glance. Ben and Molly exchanged surprised looks when the woman in the car drove away.

Robin reached down in the neck of her shirt and withdrew a chain and key. She unlocked the front door, stepped inside, and closed the door behind her.

Ben and Molly stayed in the parked car for over half an hour, but there was no sign of activity. No one came in or went out.

"I guess we'd better go," Molly said finally. "You think she's in there by herself?"

"How can we tell? My guess is that she is. Pat said that Robin has a baby-sitter on the days we don't have the camp, but, I suppose, on other days, Robin just waits at home alone until her father gets there. I don't see how we can learn anything this way," Ben said.

Molly shook her head dejectedly. "I know. I don't know what I was expecting. Maybe I was hoping some evil, awful-looking person would appear, and we'd make a report to the authorities who would apprehend him or her, and that would solve Robin's problems, and she'd start being a normal, happy little kid. Dumb, huh?"

Molly expected Ben to laugh. Ben had been laughing at Kristi and Molly's ideas and plans ever since she could remember. But this time

Ben reached over and patted her on the shoulder.

"It's not dumb," he said. "Too simple, maybe. The trouble with life is that it's a lot more complicated than we want it to be."

Molly put the car in gear and drove toward Ben's house.

"What now?" she asked.

"I guess it can't hurt to do this a couple more days, see if they go through the same routine every day. Maybe we'll think of something else by then," Ben remarked.

"Thanks for going along with me," Molly said, when she pulled into his driveway. "I really appreciate it."

He suddenly looked embarrassed. "That's OK," Ben mumbled. "I wasn't going to be doing much else anyway. Besides, I should be thanking you for giving me a lift today."

"I'll pick you up again in the morning. About the same time?"

"You sure you don't mind?"

"I'm sure. Besides, if I'm going to play Sherlock Holmes, I need a Dr. Watson."

He grinned at her, the temporary embarrassment gone.

"I'll be your Dr. Watson, Molly Kincaid," Ben said.

"Thanks," Molly said. "Something tells me I need all the help I can get. Goodbye, Watson."

"Goodbye, Holmes," he countered. Molly tooted her car horn and drove off.

The next two days were just like Monday. Several minutes after three o'clock Mrs. Perkins would pick up Robin and drop her off at the house on Spring Street. No one else seemed to be at the house.

"Tomorrow we'll try something else," Molly said when she was dropping Ben off at his house on Wednesday.

"Like what?" Ben asked.

"I'll think of something," she said airily. "Now that we've gotten the lay of the land, it's time to take action."

"Do you plan on giving me any hints ahead of time?"

"When I know, you'll know," Molly answered honestly.

"Fantastic," Ben replied.

"See you in the morning," she said.

He shoved his hands in his pockets and stood watching her from the lawn.

"You have that look on your face again," she called through the open window.

He was startled by her comment. "What?"

"There's a way you look sometimes. You know, kind of wistful."

"Gee. I hardly know how to thank you," Ben said, blushing. "Actually, I was trying to think up a different way to say thanks for the rides to work. I'm still working on that car; I'll have her running soon."

Molly looked doubtfully at the shabby car. It didn't look very good. If anything, it looked more forlorn than ever. While she admired Ben's faith, she doubted that anything could put that car into shape.

"I'll do it, Molly," he said softly.

Her eyes widened as she looked back at Ben. He had a disconcerting way of seeming to read her thoughts just at the time when she'd rather they weren't read.

"If you love that car that much, then I think you're doing the right thing by sticking with it. If you gave up on it without trying everything, you'd always regret it," Molly told him.

He smiled quietly and looked pleased.

"You understand, don't you? Somehow I didn't think you would, but I can tell you do. I'm going to have to stop thinking of you as a kid like Kristi. You've been doing some growing up on me," he said.

97

"It happens to everyone sooner or later, Ben. Even us kids."

He shook his head. "Some people never grow up," he countered.

"I don't blame them," Molly blurted out. "It's kind of scary to think I have to be responsible for everything I do and say without having the excuse of being 'just a kid.'"

Ben looked at her for a long moment. Then he said, "I know what you mean. It is scary."

Molly felt flustered. "I should go, Ben," she said, backing the car up.

"Goodbye, Molly," he called.

Molly drove on home wondering why she could talk to Ben so easily. Was it because he didn't make fun of her the way he used to? Or was it because he was curious about everything? Also, he was totally unconcerned about what everyone else did and said. With him, she decided, it was safe to be herself. When the summer was over, she would probably hardly see him. He would go back to the academy, and she would only see him in passing at the Jackson house.

She tried to dismiss thoughts of Ben from her mind and concentrate on the problem of Robin James. *There simply has to be a way*, she thought, *to get that kid to open up. Maybe Ben will come up with an idea.* He was smart, and he cared about people. She knew she could count on him. With that comforting thought, she concentrated on the short drive home.

was kind, and pleasant about people. She
... she could ... on him. With that ...
... her clothes were somehow on the
... about her there ...

# Chapter Nine

Molly woke up on Thursday feeling hot and sticky. The air was so still that the sheer organdy curtains in her bedroom hung limply, hardly stirring.

She showered slowly, wondering if Kristi would be going to the pool with all their other friends that day. Because she worked weekends at the mall, Kristi had Thursdays and Fridays off. Molly pictured herself there. The pool would be sparkling blue and clear. She would stretch out next to the water in a suit she had only worn twice during the summer. Whenever she was hot she would swim a few laps, and then climb out, the water glistening on her tanned arms and legs.

*Snap out of it, Molly*, she told herself. She

toweled off and slipped on the coolest clothes she could find, a pink tank top and thin white cotton shorts. She was sweating by the time she tied her sneakers. *It's going to be a long, hot day*, Molly told herself.

By midmorning Molly's predictions had proven only too true. As the sun rose higher in the sky, tempers flared. The humidity made everyone irritable, even the quietest children in her group. No one wanted to work on crafts.

"Why don't we all go over to the drinking fountain," Molly suggested finally. "And splash some cool water on our faces. Then we'll decide if we want to work on crafts, or do something else."

"I want juice," Amy demanded.

"Amy, we'll have juice at lunchtime. We'll have water now," Molly told her.

"I want juice," David said. Molly could see that the others were going to ask for juice if she didn't distract them soon.

"You know the rules—" she started to say, but she was interrupted by loud voices. They all turned to see what was going on.

"You're stupid!" yelled one of the older boys.

"And fat!" added a tall girl with a ponytail. All of the ten-year-olds had surrounded their counselor Paul and were calling him names. Molly wondered if she should try to intervene.

The situation looked out of control. Then a shrill whistle pierced the air. *Uh-oh*, Molly thought.

Pat was at Paul's side in a few brisk strides.

"What's going on here?" she demanded. "Paul?"

"Kevin and Martha and I were having a little discussion, Pat," Paul said. "I'm sorry that our voices got so loud."

"It sounded like more than just a discussion to me," Pat said. "Who was calling Paul names?" Everyone looked down. Molly noticed that her group, too, had quieted down since Pat had shown up.

"All right. Paul, I'm sure you're doing a good job. This group doesn't seem to understand that as the oldest ones here they have to set an example for the younger ones. If there's another outburst like the one I just heard, you'll all go home, and you won't be allowed to come back. Am I clear?" Pat asked. No one moved. "Good." She hurried back to her own group.

"How do you kids feel about going to the water fountain?" Molly asked her group. Amy stood up meekly and took Molly's hand. The rest of them walked slowly alongside. As they passed Paul's group, Molly saw several of the

103

older kids look angrily at Paul. *The day isn't over yet*, she thought.

Several smaller quarrels broke out during the rest of the day, but nothing major occurred until most of the kids had gone home.

Molly and Ben were climbing into Molly's little car when Paul came running over.

"Have you seen my keys?" he asked them. Molly shook her head. So did Ben. "My car keys. You're sure?"

"No, Paul, I really haven't seen them," Molly said.

"My dad is going to kill me if I call him at work to bring over the extra set."

"Molly and I'll help you look around for them," Ben said. "When did you last see them?"

"I don't have pockets in these shorts," Paul said. "So I put my keys with my lunch bag. But now that I think about it, I didn't see them at lunch."

"We can look around that area," Molly suggested.

"I already did. Believe me, I looked. I hate to say this"—Paul paused—"but I think one of my kids took them."

"They wouldn't do that," Ben said.

"I think Paul might be right," Molly said. "I saw the looks they were giving you. They probably hid them as a joke and then forgot all about them."

"I guess I'll just have to search the grounds," Paul muttered.

"We'll all search, Paul," Molly said. "Don't worry, they'll turn up."

"Thanks," Paul answered gratefully.

Half an hour later there was no sign of the keys, and the three of them were ready to give up.

"If they dug a hole and buried the keys, we'll never find them," Paul said.

"I think we should wait until tomorrow to see if one of the kids knows where the keys are," Ben said. "If it was just a prank, they'll be anxious to get them back to you."

"Can you give me a ride home, Molly?" Paul asked. "It would save me a call to my dad."

"Sure," Molly said. "Let's go." Just then she saw a flash of pink in a space between some gnarled tree roots.

"I didn't find your keys," she said to Paul. "But I did find a Strawberry Shortcake lunch box." She picked it up, and the three of them walked back to the parking lot.

Alicia was leaning against her white Trans Am in the parking lot. Molly wondered how she managed to look so fresh when the rest of them were so wilted and limp.

"Need a ride home, Ben?" she asked sweetly.

Molly couldn't believe her eyes. Alicia was flirting with Ben—and she wasn't being very subtle about it, either. Ben didn't seem to notice.

"Thanks for the offer," Ben said. "But Molly and I have something planned after we drop Paul off at his house."

"But how are you all three going to get in there?" Alicia asked, wide-eyed, looking down at Molly's small car. It was a two seater.

"Oh," Paul said flatly. "I'd forgotten about that. Look, Molly, I'll just give my dad a call."

Alicia's eyes never left Ben's face.

"Ben?" she asked. "Last chance."

Molly noticed that Alicia didn't offer Paul a ride home.

Molly knew that Alicia and Ben went to school together. But she wouldn't have thought Ben was Alicia's type. Alicia was beautiful, glamorous, perfect; Ben was studious, casual to the point of being sloppy—he was Ben.

"I appreciate the offer, Alicia. Maybe another time," Ben said. Alicia smiled, got into her car, and drove off.

"Well, I certainly don't rank with her," Paul commented.

Ben laughed. "Oh, Alicia's just a little self-centered, that's all. She's really all right. Let's go."

Ben squeezed into the tiny storage space behind the seats in the little car. But it was for a good cause—and for a short distance.

"We'll talk to the kids tomorrow, Paul. Cheer up," Ben said as Paul climbed out of the car at his house.

"Thanks, pal. I'll remember that." He slammed the door and walked up his driveway.

Ben flexed the muscles in his arms and stretched his thin, lanky legs. "Now I know how a pretzel feels."

"Don't complain. You could have gone with Alicia."

"Forget it. We have plans, remember? And, by the way, since the subject has arisen, what is our plan of action?"

Molly glanced at the Strawberry Shortcake lunch box next to her. A plan was beginning to take shape in her mind.

"We're going to return Robin's lunch box. She'll need it for tomorrow, don't you think?" Molly asked Ben.

"How do you know it's Robin's?" he asked.

Molly smiled. "As a matter of fact, it isn't hers. She always brings her lunch in a paper bag."

"But we don't know that, do we?"

"No, we'll ask Robin," Molly said.

"You are a master sleuth," Ben told her.

"So, you'll help?"

"I'm game. Lead the way, Holmes."

"You can call me Sherlock, my dear Watson," Molly said. "Hey, what'll we do if there's someone there besides Robin?"

"We just say we thought this was her lunch box and leave," Ben said.

Molly's heart was beating rapidly by the time they knocked at the door of Robin's house.

"Who's there?" Robin asked, her voice barely audible through the closed door.

"You tell her," Molly whispered, poking Ben in the ribs. "She likes you."

Ben nodded. "Robin," he said loudly, "it's Ben and Molly from the park. We have something we think you lost at the park."

"I didn't lose anything."

"Are you sure?" he asked. "We came all the way from the park just to ask you. Won't you at least talk to us? If you aren't supposed to let people in, we understand, but can't you come out here and talk to us?"

Robin opened the door slightly and peered out at them. Her manner was anything but friendly.

"We thought this was yours," Molly said, holding up the colorful lunch box.

Robin shook her head.

Peering through the narrow crack, Molly said, "Do you know who this lunch box *does* belong to? Ben and I would really like to get it to the right person."

"Who cares? They can use a paper bag, like me," Robin said. "I just throw it away after I've eaten."

Molly looked at Ben. She felt totally helpless.

Ben stepped closer to the crack in the door, through which Robin watched them. "Hey, Robin, why can't you come out and be friendly? We thought we were doing you a favor—"

Robin quickly interrupted him. "I don't need favors. Not from anyone."

"I need people to do favors for me once in a while. So does Molly. We all need favors sometimes. Are you mad at us?" Ben asked her. "Or maybe you've been told not to talk to people when you're home alone. We'll leave if you want. We don't want to get you in trouble."

Robin opened the door a little wider. Molly and Ben could see all of her.

"No one tells me what to do," she announced. "I can talk to anyone I want. If I wanted you to come to a tea party, I could have one right now. But I don't want to."

Molly watched as Ben tried not to smile. He was getting to Robin.

Ben said, "A tea party, huh? Well, I don't blame you for not wanting to have a tea party. They are a lot of trouble. Although I *do* like crumpets. Do you serve crumpets with the tea when you have a tea party?"

"What?" Robin asked, caught off guard.

Ben continued to sail through his line of nonsense. "Do you like crumpets for tea, Molly?" Ben asked, winking at her.

Molly decided to join in Ben's game. In a clipped British accent, she replied, "Actually, old chap, I prefer a few biscuits with my tea. I say, is this young lady inviting us to tea?"

"I'm afraid not, my dear," answered Ben. "The way I understand it, she doesn't like us well enough to invite us to tea."

Molly grinned. Ben sounded properly put out.

Robin swung the front door fully open. She looked from Ben to Molly. "I don't have any tea," Robin said.

"Even a spot of Kool-Aid would be welcome on such a hot day," Ben said, looking away from Robin's watchful eye.

Robin nodded. "I have Kool-Aid. It's cherry.

And Oreos." She hesitated. "Do you really want some?"

Ben dropped the British accent. "Are you sure you don't mind?"

Robin shook her head. She motioned for them to follow her and led them through the small house to the kitchen. Molly noticed that the house was clean and neat, but it seemed big and empty for one seven-year-old girl.

Robin seemed almost happy as she took the bag of cookies from the cabinet and placed it on the table. She carefully put ice in three glasses and poured Kool-Aid from a pitcher that had been in the refrigerator.

"That lunch pail," she said slowly, dragging out the words as if she were making a very confidential statement, "belongs to Megan Taylor. *Everything* she has is Strawberry Shortcake."

"I think you're right," Molly told her. "Now that you mention it, I've seen Megan with it. You're very observant, Robin."

Robin shrugged off the compliment. The three of them stood in silence, sipping Kool-Aid and eating Oreos.

"Where'd you learn to talk like that?" she finally asked Ben.

Ben laughed. "We were just acting silly. I guess I think it's fun to try to talk like different people and with different accents. You wanna hear my Texas talk?"

Robin nodded.

"I sure do think you've rustled up some fine grub, Miss Robin," Ben said.

Robin laughed. "More," she demanded.

"Shoot. That's easy," Ben drawled. "Me and Miss Molly would sure like you to talk to us at the park, just about anytime you got troubles, OK?"

Robin looked down at the table. Then she nodded.

"Well, that's just real fine," Ben assured her. "Mighty fine."

Then in his normal voice Ben said, "Molly, maybe we should get going. Robin, we'll see you tomorrow. Thanks for asking us in; the tea party was great."

"Even if we didn't have those crump—those things?" she asked, a small smile wavering at the corners of her mouth.

Ben said firmly, "Crumpets are, in my opinion, not very good."

Molly added, "Oreos are much better. After such a hot day at the park, I needed them. I hope you don't get in trouble for asking us in."

Robin shook her head and looked at Molly defiantly. "I won't get in trouble. My dad wants me to have friends, but I don't have any. Kids don't like me, and I don't like them."

Molly wanted to tell Robin that other kids would like her if she let them know her, but she decided not to. It wasn't the right time. A glance from Ben told her he felt the same way. The kid *had* opened up a bit. Robin needed time to decide if she trusted Molly and Ben. Molly could wait.

That night as Molly tried to go to sleep, her thoughts were not only on Robin, but also on Alicia and the way she had flirted with Ben earlier that day. The first thing Molly had thought was that Ben wasn't Alicia's type. But was Alicia Ben's type? Molly remembered the mental list she'd made—Alicia was beautiful, glamorous, and perfect. After the way Alicia had treated Paul, Molly added another word: nasty. Then, sleepily, she ran over the list she'd made up for Ben. Studious and casual to the point of being sloppy. But she'd seen other sides to Ben in the last few days. She'd have to add a couple of words to that list, too: witty and caring.

Molly turned over and snuggled into her pillow, still thinking of Ben. That afternoon after she'd dropped him off at his house, she had looked in the rearview mirror and seen him smiling at her as she drove off.

*One more word*, Molly thought as she drifted off to sleep—*cute. Definitely cute.*

# Chapter Ten

Molly woke up on Saturday, stuck her tongue out at the clock, and turned over in bed.

"Are you getting up already?" asked Kristi sleepily from the other bed.

Molly had forgotten that Kristi had spent the night at her house.

"No," Molly said emphatically. "It's Saturday, and I can stay in bed as long as I want."

"Me, too," declared Kristi. "When I had to work a double shift last week, I hated it. Now I'm glad Irene gave me a Saturday off in return."

"Some Saturdays I sleep until noon," Molly said.

"The latest I've ever stayed in bed is eleven," Kristi said. "I get too hungry."

"Mom made some cinnamon rolls," Molly volunteered. "We can sleep as late as we want and warm them up later in the microwave."

"Well, happy dreams," Kristi said.

"See you a little later," Molly said, yawning.

Molly and Kristi settled back under the sheets. They lay there for quite a while, very still.

"Molly?" Kristi said quietly.

"What?"

"What kind of cinnamon rolls did your mother make?" she whispered.

"Big ones. The kind where the dough is rolled out, spread with cinnamon and sugar, then rolled back up. These have a caramel-nut topping on them," Molly answered.

Kristi smacked her lips in anticipation. "Now I know I can't sleep. Not with something like that waiting in the kitchen for me."

"Let's go," Molly agreed.

"I'm getting worried," Kristi admitted later after she had swallowed a bite of roll. "If you don't break down soon, I really will end up being *your* slave. That wasn't what I had in mind when I made the bet."

Molly smiled smugly. "It just goes to show

116

you don't know me as well as you think you do."

The telephone rang, and Molly picked it up quickly so it wouldn't ring again and wake up her parents. It was Paul Griffin.

"Paul!" she exclaimed. "How are you doing?"

Paul got right to the point. "I have tickets for a Phil Collins concert in Columbus," he said. "It's not till next weekend, but since it's a two-hour drive there and back—and we'd be real late getting back—I thought you might want to ask your parents about it. Do you think you'd like to go?"

Molly swallowed hard. She would *love* to go. She had just bought Phil Collins's latest album. Paul would be good company, too.

Paul said, "Molly? That's OK. You don't have to think up an excuse. I just happened to think about you. You were so nice to help me when I couldn't find my keys and all. But if you don't want to go, I understand."

"Hang on a minute, Paul," Molly said.

She looked over at Kristi. "Does going to a concert with a friend who happens, by the merest coincidence, to be a boy, count as a date?"

Kristi considered it carefully. "Are a whole

bunch of people going or just you and this friend who happens to be a boy?"

Molly spoke into the receiver. "Paul, how many tickets do you have?"

"Two," he said.

"Just the two of us," she told Kristi in a small voice.

"Then it counts as a date," Kristi said firmly. "Take your choice: win the bet or miss the concert."

"Paul, I'd love to go, but I can't," she said.

"Is it the bet?" Paul asked.

"You know about that?" Molly said.

"Sure. Doesn't everyone?"

Molly sighed. It was true. Oak Park was the kind of town where personal lives were fair game for gossip.

"Sorry," Kristi said when Molly had hung up the phone.

"It's just as well. I like Paul as a friend, but I'm not really interested in dating him. If I accepted this invitation, he'd probably misunderstand. He'd be hurt if I didn't want to go out again."

"What makes you so sure there'd be another chance?" Kristi teased.

Molly glared at her.

"Not that you'd be interested," Kristi said, "but I heard that Robert is interested in you

118

again. He told Joe, who told Carol, who told *me* that Robert's trying to get up enough nerve to ask you out. So there's hope for me to win this bet yet."

"Robert who?" Molly asked innocently. They burst out laughing.

On Monday morning Molly walked out to get in her car. As she reached for the door, she heard a honk, and looking out toward the street, she saw Ben Jackson's old brown car. It had just as many dents and scrapes as ever, but it was clean and polished up. Ben was grinning at her from behind the wheel.

She walked slowly toward him.

"You look like the Cheshire cat," she commented. "You have her running, I see. I was just on my way to pick you up."

"I wanted to surprise you," he said. "So I've been out here a few minutes. I didn't want to take a chance on missing you. Hop in."

"What?" Molly asked.

"You heard me. Hop in. For a couple of weeks now, you've given me rides. You've used extra gas to pick me up each morning and take me home each evening. Now it's my turn," Ben said.

"Ben, really, this isn't necessary," Molly said. She wasn't sure she wanted to ride with

Ben. She liked the freedom and independence of driving her own car. She hadn't minded giving Ben rides when he needed them, but now they could go their separate ways. In separate cars.

"Sure, it's necessary," he insisted cheerfully.

Molly climbed into the car without saying another word. When they got to the park, she sat and waited for Ben to let her out on his side. But he stayed in his seat, a warm smile spreading across his face.

"What *are* you waiting for, Molly? Get out. We're here now."

"Ben, you know this door," she said impatiently. "After all this time, you *know* I can't get out until you do. Why do we go through this every time?"

Ben just smiled wider.

Realization dawned on her. "You fixed it?"

He nodded.

Molly cautiously pushed on the door handle, half expecting it to drop off in her hand. Instead, the door opened.

"I'm impressed," she admitted.

"I should hope so. It wasn't an easy job. Now stay there," Ben said. He got out of the car, walked around to Molly's side, and held the door open for her.

"Thank you," Molly said, surprised and pleased. Together they walked toward the play area.

That day, during music time, Pat asked Molly to play the guitar. They taught the children how to sing "London Bridge" as a round. Things had gone so well with Robin the week before that Molly was both baffled and discouraged when she looked up from her playing and caught Robin glaring angrily at her. *Maybe it's my imagination*, Molly thought, *but Robin always seems more troubled during the singing.* She sighed.

Molly met Ben in the parking lot at the end of the day.

"Gosh, I'm thirsty," she said as they got into his car. "I guess it was all that singing. I can't wait till I get home to get something cold to drink."

"I'm dry, too," Ben said offhandedly. "Do you have time to go somewhere for a soda or something? I wanted to talk to you about Robin, and I didn't have a chance at work."

"Sure, why not?" Molly answered.

Ben took her to a drive-in and ordered large sodas. He gave the waitress enough money to cover Molly's drink.

Molly had opened her purse, but Ben held up his hand and said, "Your turn next time."

Molly nodded. It crossed her mind that she was practically committing herself to another time. That didn't really bother her. In fact, she liked having the chance to talk with Ben without ten kids competing for his attention.

"I talked to Pat again about Robin," Ben said. "She wanted me to pass the information along to you. Mrs. Perkins, the woman who picks Robin up, used to take Robin to her house after three o'clock, but Robin didn't like it there. Now she stays by herself—she's only alone for an hour or so, and the lady next door keeps an eye out for her."

Molly took a long sip of her soda and watched Ben as he spoke. He wasn't really handsome, not the way Robert was. Ben, with his gray eyes and curly, tousled hair, was striking in a different way. His skin was tanned from working in the park, emphasizing the whiteness of his teeth. When Ben talked about something, Molly had to listen to him. He became so involved in his subject that he forced her to be involved, too. Kristi was lucky—although she wouldn't admit it—to have Ben as an older brother. "It was simpler your way," Molly admitted, forcing herself back into the conversation. "I should have known that Pat could find out about the kids more easily than we could. I was just too dumb to think about asking her."

"That's not dumb, Mol. So many kids come to the summer program that Pat can't possibly know each one's life story. And I liked your way of finding out things."

"You did?" she asked.

"Sure. It was fun to be Watson to your Holmes."

"Or Laurel to my Hardy," she commented.

"The way we did what we did was OK," Ben said. "I meant it when I said it was fun. We got to have a few laughs, play detective, and help Robin all at the same time. If there's a way to get a job done and have a good time in the process, that's the best way."

"So where do we go from here?" Molly asked.

"I guess that we just keep trying to show Robin that we're her friends," he said quietly. "But what I wanted to tell you was my theory, now that I've had time to think it over."

"You have a theory? I'm listening," Molly said.

"Robin probably never understood why her mother and sister left. I mean, it seemed sensible to the parents to each take a child. But maybe Robin feels that her mother didn't love her as much as she did her sister. She's mad that her mother went away. Maybe she's afraid to like or love anyone—because it hurts so much when they leave. Does that make any sense to you?"

Molly nodded. It made a whole lot of sense to her. "But why doesn't her father talk to her?" she asked.

Ben's voice was gentle when he replied, "You have to remember, Molly, that not everyone is alike. And both of them are hurting. He's probably doing the best he can."

"How'd you become so understanding?" she asked, her head tilted to one side. "You're not *that* much older than I am."

"I read a lot of dog and horse stories," he said, a blank expression on his face. "Ready to go?"

"Ready," Molly said, laughing.

During the drive home, Molly had an idea. As Ben pulled up in front of her house, she said, "You know what we ought to do, Ben?"

"What's that?"

"Well, you said we should show Robin that we're her friends. Why don't we check with her father and see if it's OK to take her out somewhere for a sundae or something. You think she'd like that?"

Ben leaned across the space that separated them and kissed her lightly on the cheek.

"What was that for?" Molly demanded.

"Because I like you, Molly Kincaid. I like you and your determined efforts on Robin's behalf," he said easily.

"Is that a compliment? Am I supposed to thank you?" Molly asked.

"Of course not. You're always surprising me, Molly," Ben said. "I've known you for years, but I never really knew you at all."

"You're pretty surprising yourself, Ben," Molly said. "See you in the morning," she added, getting out of the car. It wasn't until he'd driven off that Molly realized that he would probably pick her up in the morning. She hadn't told him not to.

"You're awfully quiet," Molly's father observed after dinner. "Have a rough day?"

Molly shook her head. "It wasn't rough, really. Just different."

"How's that?"

"I don't know," Molly said. "Things just seem different. Maybe I'm tired and don't know it or something. Maybe I'll go take a nice bubble bath and see what that does for me."

"Don't soak too long," he joked. "You're already acting like a wet noodle."

"Hey, Dad, I can't be totally 'up' all the time," Molly said defensively.

"Can this be love?" he sang.

Molly rolled her eyes. "Love? I *told* you I'm done with boys, dating, and love. I'm not even dating anyone."

"You see a lot of Ben Jackson," he pointed out.

"*Ben*? I work with Ben."

"You don't like him?" Mr. Kincaid asked.

"Sure, I *like* him. But that's totally different from wanting him for a boyfriend. Forget it, Dad. Your imagination is working overtime," Molly said. She went into the bathroom and turned on the water. Her father had been skeptical about her giving up boys. And all the weeks she hadn't been dating couldn't change his mind.

Molly shut the water off and stepped into the tub. Ben had kissed her. But it wasn't a real kiss, she told herself.

It occurred to Molly as she sank down into the scented bubbles that what was bothering her was not Ben's friendly little kiss on the cheek—it was her reaction to that kiss. She had liked it. She liked the moment of intimacy between them.

Molly drained the tub and dried herself, slipped on her white cotton nightgown, and went to her bedroom. She switched off the overhead light and lay down in her bed, cloaked in darkness.

126

She recalled the way Ben had smiled at her a few nights earlier. She had decided then that he was cute. She loved watching him with the kids at the park, whether he was answering silly questions with his own brand of nonsense or offering serious explanations about nature and science. She had always admired Ben Jackson, but everybody in town admired Ben Jackson—especially when he was on one of his crusades. Some of Molly's friends at school made fun of Ben's drive and concerns, but Molly had never been able to bring herself to agree with them. *But I never defended him, either*, she thought, suddenly ashamed.

Molly turned over on her stomach, stuffing the pillow under her chin. Her thoughts went to Robin. Robin seemed to know a lot about hurt for a seven-year-old. Molly sat up in bed. *Robin.* If Robin was afraid to love anyone again, for fear they'd leave her, what was Molly doing? Was that the key? Was that why she had to reach out to Robin? She swore off boys after what Robert had done, and Robin had sworn off *everyone*. *But it's different for me*, Molly thought. *I'm almost an adult. I made a rational decision*. She leaned back against her pillows. Robin was just a little girl. Molly *had* to help her.

# Chapter Eleven

"I'll have raspberry ice cream, blueberry sauce, hot fudge, and four maraschino cherries," Ben said.

"Yuck," Robin said quietly. Molly could hardly see the little girl over the enormous menu. She was sitting across from Ben and Robin, trying to decide between the caramel nut fudge sundae or a bowl of peppermint stick ice cream.

"I'm sorry, sir," the waiter said congenially. "We only have raspberry frozen yogurt, and the blueberries are extra."

Ben winked at Molly. "We're going to need a few more minutes to decide, then." The waiter left, and Ben turned to Robin. "Did I hear you say 'yuck' about my order?" he demanded.

Robin's head bobbed up and down, but she didn't speak.

"Molly, did my order deserve a 'yuck' from Robin?" Ben said.

"No," Molly said, looking at Robin. "I think 'gross' was probably a better word." She saw Robin stifle a smile and then look at Ben. *Gotcha*, Molly thought.

Ben held up his hands. "OK, OK, I get the message. I suppose I'll just have some vanilla ice cream. No syrup. No whipped cream. No spoon."

Robin laughed out loud. Molly's eyes opened in surprise, but Ben didn't show any sign that he'd noticed.

"No dish?" he added, glancing at Robin. She giggled and nodded. "No cone?"

The waiter returned. "Are we ready here?" he asked impatiently.

"I am," Molly said. "I'll have a dish of peppermint stick ice cream, with marshmallow on it." The waiter scribbled on his pad, then turned to Ben. He looked at Robin.

"Would I hear any complaints if I ordered a banana split, with no bananas?" Robin shook her head. "Then I'll have a banana split, hold the bananas," Ben told the waiter.

The waiter looked pointedly at Robin. She didn't say anything, so Ben prodded her. "Do you like chocolate? Strawberries? You can have anything."

Robin glanced at Molly. "I want what she's having," she said.

"Two peppermint stick ice creams with marshmallow?" the waiter inquired. Robin nodded, her eyes cast down. Molly felt as if she had scored a major victory.

Under the table Molly felt Ben's foot tread lightly on her own. Robin was still studying the tabletop. Molly gazed into Ben's eyes. She felt a warmth spread through her as she smiled back at him. And while most of her happiness centered on Robin, Molly was aware that part of it was because of her blossoming friendship with Ben.

"I almost cried when Robin laughed out loud," Molly said after they had dropped Robin off at her house. "You really did it."

"It was just the right time and the right place," Ben said.

"It was the right person, and you know it, Ben Jackson," Molly countered, punching him in the arm. "That's why you look so pleased with yourself."

"Well, some guys make touchdowns, and other guys own flashy cars. I like to make kids

131

smile. Just shows you what a geek I am," he said.

"You're not a geek," Molly said indignantly. "What made you say that?"

"I thought a lot of my old friends felt that way," Ben said.

"Then they aren't real friends," Molly said angrily. "Anyone who knows you can't think of you as a geek."

Ben looked over at Molly. "Usually I don't care what people think about me. But sometimes," he said, staring right at Molly, "I care a great deal."

Over the next few weeks a pattern developed for Ben and Molly. They started car pooling to and from work. After work they always went to Skip's for a cold drink and snack. They didn't talk about it ahead of time, it just became a part of their routine.

One hot Tuesday in early August, Molly was gathering up her things when she saw Ben and Alicia a few yards away. They were engaged in earnest conversation. Molly couldn't hear anything they said.

"I can't go for a soda or anything today," Ben said to Molly casually as he slipped behind the wheel of his car. "We'll make it up tomorrow and have two sodas, OK?"

"Sure," she said, trying to match his casual tone. She was a little disappointed. "Is something wrong?"

Ben shook his head. "Nothing at all. Alicia just asked me to help her out. She has two tickets for a rock musical in Cleveland tonight, and her date had to cancel at the last minute. Alicia asked me to go along as a favor to her."

"That's noble of you," Molly said sarcastically.

Ben shot her a surprised look, and Molly blushed. She hadn't meant her comment to sound so biting. She tried to laugh it off by saying, "A free ticket to a rock musical is not exactly punishment, Ben." Silently she added, *And neither is a date with Alicia Martin.*

"Actually," Ben said, "I've never learned to like events like that. I prefer a good stereo and good company."

"Alicia is pretty good company," Molly said. "A date always makes things nicer."

"A date? It isn't a date. I'm just filling in for a guy who didn't show up," Ben said.

They had arrived at her house. Molly said, "Have a good time tonight; I'll pick you up in the morning." She waved at him as he drove off. She wanted to kick his tailpipe.

*What is the matter with me?* she wondered.

In the privacy of her room, she consulted her reflection in the mirror. She was the picture of health. So why did she feel so rotten?

Molly flopped down on her bed. *Admit it, Kincaid*, she thought. *You're jealous.*

Molly kept reciting a few sentences over and over in her head: *Ben isn't interested in Alicia. Alicia isn't interested in Ben. Even if they were interested in each other, it wouldn't matter to me because I'm not interested in Ben.* Molly hadn't forgotten her bet with Kristi. Even if Ben asked her out, she'd have to turn him down. But he hadn't asked her out.

The next morning when Ben got into her car, Molly was bright and cheerful. "Enjoy the show?"

"It was OK. We had a pretty good time."

"That's great," she said. She had wanted him to say that he had a miserable time.

During lunch break at the park, Molly decided to eat her sandwich in the shade of a tree. Alicia Martin wandered toward her.

"How are things going today, Molly?" Alicia asked.

"Just fine. I hear you went to a pretty good musical last night."

"Fantastic," she declared. "I wasn't sure

Ben would enjoy that sort of thing, but he seemed to."

"I'm sure he did," Molly said politely. She wondered if Alicia was baiting her. They'd never had very much to say to each other.

Then Alicia looked Molly right in the eye and said, "Ben's really crazy about you, you know. I hope you're smart enough to recognize what you have in him. He's a really special guy."

Molly stared at Alicia blankly. "Come off it," she said with a laugh. "Ben and I are just friends. His sister is my best friend, and Ben's conditioned to think of us both as brats."

"That's not the way I see it," Alicia said. "I've tried all summer long to get his attention. He acts as if I don't exist."

"I don't know if he's interested in you or not," Molly said. "If he's not, it certainly isn't because of me. He's never even asked me out."

"I spent last evening with Ben, Molly. And *you* were all he talked about," Alicia said. "There are plenty of girls waiting around for a chance with him, if you don't act fast."

Molly stared down at her sneakers. *Plenty of girls waiting for a chance with Ben?*

"I like Ben," Molly said slowly. "And I think he likes me better than he used to. But I also think you're wrong, Alicia. We're friends, and that's all there is to it."

Alicia flipped back her shining hair and inspected her perfectly manicured fingernails. "I hope you're right. But I like Ben, too, Molly. When we're back at the academy this fall, I'm going to let him know it."

Molly stared at Alicia as she walked away. So Ben had mentioned her name a few times. They'd been together a lot lately, and it was only natural that he'd mention her in conversation. People could talk about other people without being in love with them. Molly walked slowly back toward the main park area, where she was going to help the kids with their crafts projects.

Molly sneaked a look over to Ben, occupied with the two brothers who shared his scientific interests.

Ben caught her staring at him and gave her a slow, sweet smile. Her heart made a strange little flip-flop.

*I'm going to call Kristi when I get home*, Molly thought determinedly. *I'll let her know that the bet is still on. No mere male, no matter how sweet his smile, will keep me from winning that bet.*

# Chapter Twelve

It was the last day of the summer park program. Molly's feelings were mixed. She was looking forward to the two free weeks she'd have before her junior year began. She wanted to swim, sleep late, and spend some of her savings on new clothes. Yet she would miss the children. She enjoyed being with them. Molly liked the sweet innocence of their friendships, the simple companionship.

She watched as Robin played underneath a tree with some of the other kids. Robin had a lot more confidence than she'd had at the beginning of the summer; she didn't hang back from the group as she once had. Molly knew that she and Ben had helped the little girl. Molly wondered if she'd ever see Robin again after that day.

Robin left the other children and walked hesitantly toward Molly. Molly smiled and sat down on the grass. She had learned not to overwhelm Robin with attention, to let Robin seek her out.

"Hello," Molly said. "What were you playing over there?"

"A dumb game," Robin said. Molly didn't say anything. "Megan made it up. It's not really dumb," Robin added.

They sat in silence, watching the different groups of kids in the park. Molly noticed Robin staring at the grass. She looked intent on something.

"Robin?" Molly said. "Did you want to talk to me?"

Robin shrugged. Then she said, "I didn't like you at first."

Molly took a breath. "That's OK, Robin. We're friends now."

"I know," Robin said. She fidgeted with a shoelace. Molly remembered the day Ben had used that shoelace to get Robin to talk. It seemed so long ago.

"I don't like that song," Robin said in a low voice.

Molly leaned closer to the little girl. Robin

was staring at her shoe and wouldn't look at Molly.

"What song, Robin?" Molly asked gently.

Robin blinked twice. A tear slid down her nose and landed with a plop on her tennis shoe. Molly wanted to hug the little girl to her, but instinctively she kept her hands at her sides.

"What song is it that you don't like, Robin?" Molly repeated. "I wouldn't have sung it if I'd known."

"The bear song," Robin whispered. "The bear and the mountain."

"The Bear Went Over the Mountain"? Molly remembered the first day she'd sung it. That was the day Robin had told her that she was ugly and that Molly couldn't sing as well as Robin's mother could.

With sudden insight, Molly asked softly, "Did your mother sing that song, Robin?" Robin nodded and looked at Molly, her eyes brimming with tears.

"I didn't know," Molly said. "Oh, Robin, I'm sorry."

"*I'm* sorry," Robin said. "I wasn't very nice to you."

"It's really all right," Molly said. "I know that your mother doesn't live with you anymore. But, Robin, I know that she loves you and that she wants to be with you as much as you want to be with her."

"That's what Daddy says," Robin told her. "I'm going to see her next week."

Molly smiled. "Oh, I'm so glad. And when you come back, call me. You and Ben and I still have to go out for ice cream every now and then, all right?"

Robin nodded and stood up. "I'll be right back," she said. "Get Ben." She ran over to the picnic area. Molly got to her feet and looked around for Ben. He was walking toward her.

"We're supposed to stay here," Molly told him. "Robin asked me to make sure to get you and wait for her."

"I'm going to miss this bunch, aren't you?" Ben asked. Molly didn't have to answer.

Robin ran up to them. She handed Ben a pocket comb in a leather case with bright stitching up the sides. "I made this in crafts," she said. "So you'll remember me."

"Thank you, Robin," Ben said. "I like it a lot, but I don't need anything to make me remember you. Anyway, I'll see you again."

"That's what I told her," Molly said.

"And this is for you," Robin told Molly. She held out a small box. Molly looked at it. It was covered with pink shells. On the lid Robin had pasted white shells in the shape of an *M*.

"I made it at home for you," Robin said shyly. "So you'd be surprised."

A lump came to Molly's throat. She swallowed hard.

"It's beautiful. I'm going to use it to keep my very favorite earrings in."

She bent down to hug Robin, who threw her arms around Molly's neck.

"You promise to stay in touch?" Molly asked.

"Yes," Robin promised. Then she skipped off to join Jennifer and Megan.

Ben gave Molly's hand a quick squeeze. "Excellent work, Holmes," he said to Molly.

"I couldn't have done it without you, my dear Watson," Molly replied. She was afraid that she was going to cry.

Ben winked at her, squeezed her hand again, and went over to talk to Paul. Molly stared down at her hand. She felt suddenly alone. Ben? She *couldn't* be feeling that way about Ben. But the truth was the truth: she *was* feeling that way, and it *was* about Ben.

At home that afternoon Molly felt restless. The whole summer had been structured. Now she suddenly had two free weeks stretching ahead of her.

"I think I'll take a drive through town," she

told her mom. "I have this urge for a hot fudge sundae before dinner. I'll be back in a while."

Molly drove to Skip's. Ben had turned down her offer to buy him a soda after work. He had barely spoken to her on the way home.

Molly sat down in a booth by herself and ordered her sundae. Right after she ordered, Robert Prentiss walked in. Molly immediately noticed how great he looked. His hair was stylishly windblown; his shirt and pants emphasized his muscular build. He looked Molly's way and nodded. She smiled back.

Robert seemed to take her smile as encouragement. He walked over to her booth. "Mind if I sit with you?" he asked. He sounded nervous.

"Suit yourself," she said. She was surprised at how detached she felt from him and the situation.

"Did you have a good summer?" he asked.

"As a matter of fact, I did," Molly said. "I'd do it again in a minute." She looked at Robert. "How did *your* summer go?"

"So-so, I guess. I worked for my dad some. Molly?" he asked.

"Yes?"

"About what happened with us last spring, I'm sorry. I guess I was flattered because Linda kept after me. But I've been sorry ever since then that I didn't patch things up at the time."

"Why didn't you?" she asked, looking him right in the eyes. The whole conversation should have thrilled her. Instead, Molly found she was almost bored.

"I don't know," he mumbled. "Pride, I guess. You told me off in front of all our friends. I couldn't just run after you and apologize. But now I wish I had. I've been trying to find an opening all summer, but there never was one."

Molly just stared at Robert. How much time did he spend getting his hair to look so perfect? she wondered.

Robert continued. "I think this is the first time in weeks I've seen you alone. You always have someone with you. Usually that Ben Jackson," Robert said scornfully.

"What about Ben?" she flared up. "He's a good friend and a really nice guy."

Robert looked skeptical.

"I wondered about it when I kept seeing you with him. The way you looked at him and everything. But I hoped I was wrong. That he was just a friend."

"That's the way it is," Molly replied mildly. "We aren't going together. We've never even had a date."

He reached across the booth to cover both of her hands with his. "Molly," he began earnestly, "if that's true, will you consider going with me again? I meant it when I said I regret what happened."

"That's OK, Robert," she said. "I think my pride was more hurt than anything else. We can be friends now. No hard feelings."

"Then you'll go with me?" His face lit up all over, and he continued to hold her hands.

She shook her head. "No, I don't feel the same way now as I did then. Sometimes I think I must be a totally different person. As I said, there are no hard feelings, but—" She stopped, looking everywhere but at Robert. Then she saw Ben, coming through the door of Skip's. He took one glance in her direction, saw Robert with his hands on hers and strode out.

Robert sighed. He released her hands. "I guess I'll have to accept that. If you're sure."

"I'm sure," Molly said, sliding out of the booth. She left Robert sitting there. He'd have to pay for her sundae. Molly didn't care, she knew where she was going and what she was going to do.

The expression on Ben's face when he had seen her with Robert told Molly everything she needed to know. Alicia had been trying to tell Molly the truth. Ben did love her.

Molly should have seen it sooner. She got in her car and started the engine. She let it idle for a moment while she thought. For weeks she had noticed Ben watching her, smiling at her, encouraging her. In her heart she had known that he was giving her more than brotherly attention. But then he would remind her about her bet with Kristi, and Molly would harden her resolve to win that bet, ignoring her feelings for Ben or passing them off as friendship.

Her feelings for Ben must have been written all over her face, ever since the night her father teased her about being in love. Because it was true. She loved Ben.

She drove over to the Jackson house and parked the car. Ben had a bucket of sudsy water, some brushes, rags, and the garden hose next to him. He had soaped up one battered fender of his car.

"What are you doing?" Molly asked in an innocent voice.

"Working off some energy," Ben muttered. "I can do your car next. I have a *lot* of excess energy."

"And where did all this energy come from?" Molly asked.

"Oh, it's been kind of building up all summer," Ben said. "I've been trying to help this friend of mine win a bet. I wanted her to win the bet. I really did. But I also wanted her to lose the bet," Ben added, scrubbing the front grill of his car.

"I think I know why you wanted to help her win the bet," Molly said, picking up a brush. "Why did you want her to lose it?"

"Oh, I didn't just want her to lose it," Ben said, running the hose over the grill, "I wanted to be the reason she lost the bet."

"And what happened?" Molly asked, watching Ben while she cleaned a hubcap.

"My sense of honor defeated me," Ben said. "I realized I could be the very person who would ask her to lose the bet. I couldn't do it, so I put some distance between this person and me, only to have Robert Prentiss move in on her."

"Is that how it looked?" Molly asked.

"Yes. So, did you lose?" Ben countered, facing Molly for the first time.

"Not yet. But in the next ten minutes I could be persuaded," Molly said, moving closer to Ben, "to go tell Kristi she won."

"You're not back with Robert?" Ben asked. Molly pretended to glare at him.

"I had the chance," Molly said. "But I'm

interested in someone else. Oh, Ben," Molly said, the teasing tone gone from her voice, "I don't care about him. I haven't for a long time. The only person I'd lose that bet for is—you."

Ben closed the distance between them. "You used to drive me crazy because you were a brat. Now you drive me crazy because you aren't."

Molly ignored his soapy sweat shirt and the fact that they were in full view of all the Jacksons' neighbors. When Ben leaned over and gently kissed her on the lips, Molly kissed him back with all her heart.

"I love you, Molly," Ben said into her ear. "I've loved you for a long time."

"Oh, Ben—I love you, too."

He kissed her again. "I understand you're off work for the next two weeks," he said, teasing her again. "Have you made any plans?"

"I don't know," Molly said. "I might find some time to save some whales, help sad children, and wash beat-up cars. It depends on who's asking."

"I'm asking," Ben said sternly. "I think we've accomplished enough this summer. Why don't *you* show *me* how to relax?"

"Now there's a switch," Molly teased. "Ben

Jackson, Champion of the Underdog, goes swimming." They burst out laughing.

"Ben, I have someone I have to go see now," Molly said. "By the way, I probably won't be seeing much of you in September. I'll be too busy doing Kristi's homework and ironing her clothes."

"See you in October," Ben said, winking. Molly dried off her hands on the towel nearby and went inside. Kristi was lying on the couch, thumbing through *Seventeen* magazine.

"Kristi," Molly said, lunging right in, "I have news. Robert wants me back."

"I won!" Kristi yelled, flinging the magazine aside.

"I told him no," Molly said. "I don't care about him anymore."

"I lost?" Kristi asked wonderingly. "You turned Robert down?"

"Yes," Molly answered. "But there's more."

"Somebody else?" Kristi asked triumphantly. "I knew you couldn't last. Kincaid without a boy is like peanut butter without—"

"Knock it off, Kristi. Two months ago I probably would have agreed with you," Molly said. "I proved something to myself that has changed all that. I don't need anyone else to be happy. In fact, the guy I like now knows that better than anyone. That's probably why we like each other."

"So who is it?" Kristi cried. "Come on, slave, confess!"

"Well, if I'm over here as your slave, I'm going to see a lot of him. So I don't mind being your slave," Molly said.

"Ben? It's *Ben*? I can't believe it!" Kristi shrieked. "I think I'm going to need time to get used to this."

"You'll have time," Molly said. "I have a feeling that Ben and I will give you lots of time to get used to it."

"Wait a minute," Kristi said. "Does this mean I have to be nice to him? Gosh, are he and I going to end up on double dates with you and any boy that asks me out?"

Molly laughed. "We'll work it out, Kristi." She walked over to the door. "Since I'll be your slave when school starts, I have to use my free time wisely right now." Molly went out to join Ben.

Ben must have heard the door close behind Molly; he was smiling broadly as she approached the driveway.

"Is it October already?" he asked her.

"No," Molly said, stretching her arms over her head in the fading, summer light. "It's August. In another half hour this car will be

149

polished to a reasonable shine, the sun will be down, and all the stars will be out."

"It sounds like a perfect night to take the girl I love for a ride in my car," Ben said.

"I was hoping you'd say that," Molly replied, picking up a soapy sponge.

We hope you enjoyed reading this book. All the titles currently available in the Sweet Dreams series are listed on page 2. They are all available at your local bookshop or newsagent, though should you find any difficulty in obtaining the books you would like, you can order direct from the publisher, at the address below. Also, if you would like to know more about the series, or would simply like to tell us what you think of the series, write to:

Kim Prior,
Sweet Dreams,
Transworld Publishers Limited,
61–63 Uxbridge Road,
Ealing, London W5 5SA.

To order books, please list the title(s) you would like, and send together with your name and address, and a cheque or postal order made payable to TRANSWORLD PUBLISHERS LIMITED. Please allow cost of book(s) plus 20p for the first book and 10p for each additional book for postage and packing.

*(The above applies to readers in the UK and Ireland only.)*

If you live in Australia or New Zealand, and would like more information about the series, please write to:

Sally Porter,
Sweet Dreams,
Corgi & Bantam Books,
26 Harley Crescent,
Condell Park,
N.S.W. 2200,
AUSTRALIA.

Kiri Martin,
Sweet Dreams,
c/o Corgi & Bantam Books New Zealand,
Cnr. Moselle and Waipareira Avenues,
Henderson,
Auckland,
NEW ZEALAND.

# WINNERS

## by Suzanne Rand

A great new mini-series coming soon . . .

Being seventeen can be great fun – as Stacy Harcourt, Gina Damone and Tess Belding discover as they enter their exciting senior year at Midvale High School. Apart from years of friendship, the popular trio share their main interests in common – an obsession with cheerleading in the elite school squad, and boys! For all three girls, the intricate gymnastic jumps and routines of their favourite hobby are the best things in their lives – but the gorgeous footballers they are supporting are definitely the icing on the cake! Picked to lead the cheering, the girls know they have one of the school's highest honours and a big responsibility to be the best that they can be in every way.

Each book highlights the story of one of the girls.

1. THE GIRL MOST LIKELY
2. ALL AMERICAN GIRL
3. CAREER GIRL

WINNERS – coming soon wherever Bantam paperbacks are sold!

**If you enjoy Sweet Dreams, there's a whole series of books you'll like just as much!**

# SWEET VALLEY HIGH

*Created by Francine Pascal*
*Written by Kate William*

SWEET VALLEY HIGH is a great series of books about identical twins, Elizabeth and Jessica Wakefield, and all their friends at Sweet Valley High. The twins are popular, daring and smart – but Jessica is always scheming and plotting in ways only she knows how, leaving Elizabeth to sort out the mess!

Every story is an exciting insight into the lives of the Sweet Valley High 'gang' – and every one ends on a gripping cliffhanger!

So come and join the Wakefield twins and share in their many adventures!

Here's a list of all the Sweet Valley High titles currently available in the shops:

# Caitlin

*Created by Francine Pascal*
*Written by Joanna Campbell*

From Francine Pascal, creator of SWEET VALLEY HIGH, comes her most irresistibly dazzling star – CAITLIN! She's breathtaking, captivating, outrageous and *unforgettable!*

### Book One: CAITLIN: LOVING

To everyone at her exclusive Virginia boarding school, Caitlin seems to have it all. But there is a secret need that haunts her life. A need for love. And only one boy can make her forget her cold home life, can fulfill her need for love: handsome, sensitive Jed Michaels. Jed, who has already given his heart to another girl.

### Book Two: CAITLIN: LOVE LOST

Find out what happens when the boy she loves uncovers Caitlin's darkest secret. Can their love survive!

### Book Three: CAITLIN: TRUE LOVE

And cross your fingers for Caitlin and Jed when they face a deadly danger. Can *they* survive?

### CAITLIN. THERE'S NEVER BEEN
### A HEROINE LIKE HER!